The Little Gray Notebook

Gerhard Hennes

authorHOUSE®

AuthorHouse™
1663 Liberty Drive
Bloomington, IN 47403
www.authorhouse.com
Phone: 1-800-839-8640

First published by AuthorHouse 10/13/2009

ISBN: 978-1-4490-0202-2 (sc)

Printed in the United States of America
Bloomington, Indiana

This book is printed on acid-free paper.

TO CONNIE AND RENI

– blauen sind, was für Hände sie haben
und wie sie ihr Lachen bringen, wenn blonde
Knaben die schönen Schalen bringen, von
saftigen Früchten schwer.

Eine Weihnachtsgeschichte.

Manche Weihnacht war ich draußen. Es
waren rauschende Landser- und Kasino-
weihnachten, in denen die wahre Sehnsucht
nach heimatlichem Weihnachtsglanz in
"Kameradschaftlichem Beisammensein", ge-
fühlvollem Gesang, in Strömen von Alkohol
ertränkt wurde. Da war ein Heiligabend,
an dem ein grau-staubiger Kameldorn-
busch den Weihnachtsbaum ersetzen sollte
und doch nicht konnte, an dem wir später,
mein Kraftfahrer und ich, in unserem
Wagen, der unser Zuhause war, beim Schein
einer Kerze, bei einem würzigen Glühwein
und leisen heimatlichen Radioklängen
recht still und recht allein waren. Da war
eine laute, gemacht frohe Bescherung im
Gefangenenlager, ein Schlemmen in Essen
und Trinken, und nachher ein stilles

Table of Contents

FOREWORD IX

PROLOGUE (WRITTEN IN 1946).. XI

THE SPIESSES OF THE SIEGERLAND 1

BOOK ONE: THE HUNGER YEARS

THE DEATH OF A CITY 9

HOME AT LAST 22

LITERARY INTERESTS 37

POLITICS... 41

STUDYING AND ASSESSING... 53

ARABESQUES.. 55

HEIDI 63

BOOK TWO: THE GERMAN MIRACLE

A JOB.. 77

CORNELIA AND IRENE 88

A CARE PACKAGE AND PICKLED MUSHROOMS 103

WORK: WIDENING VISTAS... 108

BAD HOMBURG 114

THE BIG CITY... 128

EPILOGUE.. 138

ABOUT THE AUTHOR 141

FOREWORD

The Little Gray Notebook is the fourth chapter in our family history from 1920 to 1943. The earlier ones were published in 2006 and 2008. Their titles were *The Barbed Wire* and *Under the Crooked Cross*.

We three boys were born well after World War I. We grew up in an ancient village east of Cologne and spent our high-school years in equally ancient Coblence, a city founded by the Romans -- Confluentia -- where the Moselle joins the Rhine River. For us, these were "the good old times," even though Hitler had come to power in 1933.

He and his party wrought major changes in society and eventually plunged the whole world into the violence, misery, destruction and death of World War II. There had never been slaughter on such a scale: some twenty million Russians and eight million Germans perished in that bloody struggle. And millions of Jews were wantonly killed -- just because they were deemed to be different.

The Little Gray Notebook covers the hungry years from 1946 to 1948, when the Marshall Plan, the currency reform and German industriousness combined to raise Germany from the ashes. That Germany was divided into east and west, along the Iron Curtain. In 1989 it was reunited. Few had expected such unification, ever. I certainly did not. But such are the sometimes surprising and even friendly turns of history.

It also describes "The German Miracle," the re-awakening of an economic giant beginning with the currency reform in June 1948.

Since then, many more years have come and gone. And I have become an old man, quite old indeed. When I was younger, I thought that, with luck, I might make the new millennium. But already, eight more years have passed.

   As I reworked this manuscript in the fall of 2008, it occurred to me that it should perhaps include an earlier essay about the Spiesses of the Siegerland, forebears on Oma's side. Make it <u>roots</u>.

PROLOGUE (written in 1946)

It must be attempted: to talk about us men, still so young and yet marked by living through a war. It is time, too, to talk about Germany, our Germany. It is like a beggar in rags. It seems so distant that it cannot be seen any more. Only rarely does it shine: in the eyes of a blond child and in the beam of sunshine that, just for a moment and surrounded by dark clouds, gilds billowing wheat fields. About us, the younger generation, and that Germany in darkness, then, let me talk.

Silence surrounds me. The small bright room is full of flowers. I am visiting with fellow POW Arthur, and his new wife. Outside under the fruit trees, in the gardens, in the fields, summer reigns. Inside, it is quiet; only the small alarm clock ticks hastily. Sometimes: a distant car, children's laughter, steps outside the house.

I look up: on the wall hangs a child's picture, drawn by Peter Paul Rubens. Do you see how the child looks ahead, over his ample cheeks and full lips; and how, completely absorbed, he might be playing with a toe, his own fingers or a jumping jack? We cannot distract the child, so preoccupied is he.

The time has come to reflect on how it all began, and where. Nobody is all of a sudden he who he is. Gradually, he has become. Many people and events have formed him: the parents; the house with forest, field and street; the years in school; perhaps an old tree, a monument, a fountain, a legend, an important event. All of these things have made him who and what he is. But I forgot something which forms a man more than anything else: war. Is war not the father of all things, the father of all of us who are young? It took a long time until we became what we are. Let me begin when we lost our Germany.

The war which was perhaps our secret longing since the winter evenings when we three boys were together, munching apples and listening to Oma reading legends of ancient heroes -- the war, our war, was lost. We could not immediately grasp that loss when we assembled the last time in full uniform. We could not comprehend when in our POW camp in Tennessee the German commandant said that, according to all news services, it is a fact that the *Führer* has died. We, the minority in my vintage who had survived the war, looked straight ahead. We did not see the hands ahead raised in salute nor the heads of others in front of us. Our eyes were focused on some distant object. There were no tears in our eyes but also no luster. In our eyes, the light had died. We were burnt out.

The fire in our eyes, unlike that in the eyes of many who had already lost their faith in Germany, had still burnt brightly, in defiance of those others, but now it had gone out. Had the *Führer* not been our last, our only hope? As long as he lived, nothing was lost. But he was dead.

We went to our barracks, in small groups, silent, and stared ahead onto the camp street and through it, to somewhere. Where, we did not know, for we had lost our sense of direction. No more goal. Things were indistinct. Was it because our eyes were suddenly moist with tears? Did the world look like this through tears? In our throats there was a lump. And a hand might wipe across the eyes. Nobody took notice. Nobody was ashamed of such weakness. We set foot before foot and looked onto the street. We searched for something that was no longer there: our Germany.

For a long time we POWs had waited for this day, the day of our discharge. It should have been a great day, to be free after almost three years of captivity, wholly free. Yet it was a day like a thousand before and a thousand thereafter. The moment we had longed for in long and lonesome nights turned out to be undistinguished and marginal: we went through a gate, some gate; we stood with our meager luggage in a street with trees, some street; we moved tired feet forward in the direction of a railroad station, some station. I thought of Father who had to stay behind. Recent weeks in our common journey as POWs had been difficult.

Why were they difficult? That is a long story. But because it belongs here I will tell it.

When we were small, we three brothers, always cheerful and equally mischievous, we called him *Vater* (Father), not Dad; just as it would never have occurred to us to call Mother "Mom." Our parents were Father and Mother, in contrast to other fathers and mothers who might be "Papa" or

"Mama." Father was a minister. To this day I do not know whether he who became a soldier in both World Wars might not have been a better soldier than pastor.

As a minister, though, he was a competent man. Members of his flock would testify to it in attitude and word. Only yesterday when Father, Mother and I were together with our former parish deaconess, she read to us a poem which talks of Father, a poem which my then grade-school teacher had written. I owe Otto Degenhard so much. He belongs to what formed me, together with the heroes' legends and the old trees in the forests surrounding our village. We had almost forgotten that poem. But here it is -- with some sentences in the rugged dialect of our native region which, alas, defy translation. It is the story of "our pastor" and his miniscule car, the Dixi, in the early thirties.

Our Pastor

Is man not like a tree with branches and with roots,
Who clings to his endeavor's space,
If large or small, and with a thousand little roots?
He simply cannot shed that place
To which belongs his mind and heart.
A thousand wounds are torn, should he depart.

At such departure, then, a happy word be spoken,
Expressing gratitude and of just praise a token.
Big words of thanks for life and duties all fulfilled
Belong to others more important to emit.
It is for me to speak of little things, distilled,
To draw the pastor's picture and to make it fit.

Was there a child to baptize on a distant mountainside
Which Oma and Opa had climbed, all out of breath and stride,
They worried yet about the homeward walk:
"Soon we'll have to be on our long way home," so goes their talk.
But who drives up, his small car crackling ever faster:
"Why, that is him, our very pastor!"

It's true: the car is smaller than "petite";
The grandparents, though, in the narrow seats they fit. --
Somewhere in the vale a wedding feast?
Is there someone with a heavy load
From shopping groceries, and on the dusty road?
Who comes, who helps to overcome a near-disaster?
"Why, who could it be, but our pastor!"

In winter gifts need distribution
To help the poorest with a just solution.
The Dixi thus became a real wheels-<u>cum</u>-chest;
Its tiny room seemed to expand beyond the rest.
A bed and mattress even shows
Protruding from its open windows.
Like with a moving van but so much faster:
The Dixi and our very pastor!

And what about our busy midwife-"aunt,"
Whose praise was in just everybody's mouth?
In quarters high it had been sealed and done:
We're sorry, but she would be gone.
Behold, the zealous wheels, they ran across the land;
A fine petition was submitted, and the verdict is in hand:
"Aunt" Anna stays; and this is right
For our <u>Heimat</u>'s future must be bright.
How come, our valley did not lose her?
"He done it, our pastor!"

Who pokes around, all flustered, in the pockets of his coat
And yet, he cannot find the key to our church's organ?
"By God, the teacher has forgot his key.
The service must begin and we must sing.
He must have left it at his home, you see.
Without the organ we simply cannot hold a tune, not you nor me."
No problem: the robe and cap are taken off,
And little Dixi hurries down the road.
The bells ring somewhat longer to await the master,
But there: pott, pott, pott - -
He's back, our nimble pastor!

A goodly number of our sick, they can report
That tiny Dixi got them to the hospital in time.
A little service, so it seems, not much ado,
Not even worth a word of thanks, it's true.
A friendly gesture, not so big a thing,
Yet should it be forgotten or should it praises bring?
It is the little things that show a person's heart the faster;
Our thanks lie in two little words: our pastor!

THE SPIESSES OF THE SIEGERLAND

The County of Gimborn, now that of Oberberg, stretches across the hilly and wooded reaches of the eastern Rhineland, some thirty to forty-five miles east of Cologne. In 1609 the County of Gimborn came to Protestant Prussia. Nestled in a valley of meadows and fields and surrounded by tall spruce forests, Wiedenest is an ancient village going back to the times of Charlemagne. From 1919 to 1934 Father was the minister in Wiedenest, where brothers Fritz (1920), Richard (1924) and I (1922) were born.

The Oberberg is a pleasant place with meandering brooks and villages with half-timbered houses and medieval churches. The native-born are a sturdy lot, combining the lighter temperament of the Rhinelander with the heavier step of the Westphalian.

To the south and east of the Oberberg, some thirty-five miles away, lies the "big" city of Siegen, with perhaps 30,000 inhabitants before World War II. Heavily damaged in that war, Siegen was an industrial hub of iron-ore mines, steelworks and large brick factories. It is the center of the Siegerland, named after the River Sieg.

In the Siegerland the mountains are higher and the valleys more deeply cut than in the Oberberg. The Siegerland is home to the large Spiess clan to which the Aulers -- Auler was the maiden name of our maternal grandmother called "Oma" -- became related by marriage. Oma's mother was a née Spiess.

With a handful of others the Spiess family -- the name was also spelled Spies -- belonged to the leading "hammersmith" clans in the Siegerland. A "hammer" is a water-driven forge. Large deposits of iron ore and rushing water combined with human brain and muscle power to make the Siegerland a place of steel manufacture long before the Industrial Revolution.

1

On July 5, 1518, the hammersmith family of Spiess was "born." On this day Count William of Nassau gave to a Hans Spiess half of the hammer at Müsenershütten as a fief in perpetuity: "We, William Count of Nassau…, herewith declare on our behalf and that of our heirs that we have donated to Hans Spiess of Bürbach, for him and his heirs and in perpetuity, half of the hammer at Mysseners near Wydenau; also a piece of fields on Caener Mountain, as well as some land, a garden and a meadow behind that garden …." The Count also proclaimed measures to make the hammer economically viable. For this right, Hans and his heirs had to pay an annual rent of six gold pieces.

The earliest references to the inhabitants of Bürbach and their properties are contained in the tax registers of the early fifteenth century. From May 1484 on, Hans (Spiess) regularly paid a May and fall tax of some 3-1/2 "albus" (probably a silver coin). The other fourteen Bürbach citizens, with a few exceptions, paid the same. From 1505 on, individual tax payers were no longer listed by name; so we lose track of Hans.

However, his son, "Hannes Spiess Soen (son) of Bürbach," operated the Müsenershütten hammer until 1546, the year of Luther's death. But he must have died around that time, because the special "Turk tax" register of 1546 records a Nachlass (inheritance or estate) of Hans the Spiess. (The Turks had laid siege to Vienna in 1529, a national crisis for the Roman Empire of the German Nation.)

When Hans died, his widow Agnes was still alive. So were his three sons: Hans the Elder, his father's successor at Müsenershütten; Hans the Younger at Dillenhütten; and Johann, later at Schneppenkauten. With these three sons begins the migration of the Spiess clan to almost all the villages of the Siegerland, indeed far beyond that region.

The Müsenershütten clan of Hans the Elder, who died around 1560, purchased additional buildings of the hammer from the Count. His descendants were so prominent in the village that Müsenershütten changed its name to Spiesshütte in the second half of the sixteenth century. The family spread across the Siegerland, and most members were blacksmiths or steel-mill workers.

The Dillenhütten clan -- Hans the Younger died in 1584 -- has lived in Büschhütten for better than four-hundred years, many male members also working as hammersmiths.

Johann Dietrich Spiess (1781-1856) of Kredenbach, one of his descendants, married Anna Gertraud Dohnleben of Bürstadt in 1807.

He was a master mason in Bürstadt with a large progeny. Under his sons Anton (1811-1886) and Wilhelm (1826-1885) the parents' house was divided. The elder son inherited the left half; from his first name the still common house name of "Andons" has taken root.

But we must get back to the sixteenth century and the Schneppenkauten clan of Johann Spies, who died around 1572. His became the largest tribe. From Schneppenkauten the family spread to Sieghütte, Siegen and above all to Gosenbach, where in 1637 Johann Spies married into the long-established Latsch family. For decades these Spiesses were tenants of the domain of the Keppel Foundation. Johann's son, Hans Wolfgang (1638-1727), had fifteen children, among them seven sons. His descendants included many hammersmiths, miners, factory workers and distributors of steel products, but also farmers, a mill owner and a famous pietist or religious "renewer."

The sons of Hans Henrich Spies (1663-1730) broke out of this age-old mold of hammersmiths and miners. One of his sons, Johann Henrich (1725-1780), became princely administrator and counsellor in Dillenburg (Nassau-Dillenburg was a branch of the House of Nassau). His nephew Johann Friedrich ascended to the position of chancellor of the church government in the same city.

In the following hundred years the descendants of these Spiesses turned to academic professions, especially in government and the Church. There are few towns between Dillenburg and Frankfurt in which, at one time or another, a Spiess was not the local pastor.

Among the descendants, too, were many important personalities, such as Johann Christoph Spiess (1771-1829), pastor and composer of church hymns; Karl Spiess (1873-1921), pastor and folklorist; Hermine Spiess (1857-1893), concert singer in Wiesbaden and friend of Johannes Brahms; Mathilde Ludendorff, née Spiess (1877-1966), religious philosopher and author; and her brother Fritz Spiess (1881-1949), an admiral and the leader of the South Atlantic Meteor Expedition.

A peculiar postscript to Mathilde Ludendorff. She was the second wife of General Erich Ludendorff (1865-1937), chief of staff to Field Marshal Paul von Hindenburg in the first half of World War I. In 1923 he participated in Hitler's attempt to overthrow the state government of Bavaria. In 1924 he became a member of the <u>Reichstag</u>; and in 1926, with his wife Mathilde, founded the Tannenbergbund, a new religious community named after the Battle of Tannenberg in 1914.

Why this extraneous postscript? Well, the Ludendorffs entered a strange and mostly one-sided discussion between a Heidelberg taxi driver and me near midnight of a long day in February 1999.

We made small talk, that non-descript taxi driver and I. I told him that I lived in America but had served in the German army in World War II. Had I read Ludendorff's book on World War I? No. "He was a great man. His book is a classic. His wife: a deep thinker and wonderful writer." My memory of Ludendorff, including his picture as a rather rotund and bemedaled general, was that of a superb strategist but also of an ambitious "politician." So I dared inject after this accolade of the Ludendorffs: "But did he not make a serious error in lending his reputation and influence to Hitler's schemes in 1923?" "Oh no, he was right. He knew where the future lay." Or words to that effect.

I took a closer look at my new friend and decided to say no more. But I extracted later that he had studied law but made better money driving a Mercedes taxi. He seemed like a "regular" guy in a leather jacket, obviously on the far right. I would have forgotten about Mathilde, Erich and him had he not pulled out of his briefcase before we parted a photocopied sheet, a gift for me, he said. There were more sheets where this one came from.

I read it the next day. Here it is. You will understand why it shook me, badly. Should I have reported the incident to the police, such propaganda being punishable by law in Germany? But I knew neither license number nor name -- and did not want to bother. To be sure, such radical and neo-Nazi groups are no more than a small fringe, in the USA as in Germany. In a way, I was glad that I was not just some innocent tourist. Still, Erich and Mathilde are not yet quite dead -- or so it seems.

NO. 10,258.

To-day's Weather:

FRIDAY, MAR

JUDEA DECLARES

Jews Of All The

BOYCOTT OF GERMAN GOODS

MASS DEMONSTRATIONS IN MANY DISTRICTS

DRAMATIC ACTION

"Daily Express" Special Political Correspondent.

ALL Israel is uniting in wrath against the Nazi onslaught on the Jews in Germany.

Adolf Hitler, swept into power by an appeal to elemental patriotism, is making history of a kind he least expected. Thinking to unite only the German nation to race consciousness is has roused the whole Jewish people to a national renaissance.

The appearance of the swastika symbol of a new Germany has called forth the Lion of Judah, the old battle symbol of Jewish defiance.

Fourteen million Jews dispersed throughout the world have banded together as one man to declare war on the German persecutors of their co-religionists. Sectional differences and antagonisms have been submerged in one common aim—to stand by the 600,000 Jews of Germany who are terrorised by Hitlerist anti-semitism, and to compel Fascist Germany to end its campaign of violence and suppression directed against its Jewish minority.

World Jewry has made up its

appealing for an end of the Hitler "terror."

Every Rabbi in the City of New York has been placed under a sacred obligation by Rabbinical decree to devote Saturday's sermon to the plight of the Jews in Germany.

The "New York Times" this morning says a list of a thousand German immigrants who have come to the United States during recent years has been compiled by an overseas Nazi organisation, the object being to use these people for Nazi propaganda in the United States.

SPECIAL SESSION

The organisation of Jewish youth in Britain is organising demonstrations in London and the provinces during the week-end.

The Board of Deputies of British Jews, representing the entire Jewish community in Great Britain, is meeting in

MARCH 24, 1933

ONE PENNY.

AR ON GERMANY

24, 1933. Hq

St IVEL CHEESE Aids digestion 2d., 6d. & 8½d. each.

Wappen der familie
Spieß (Spies)

BOOK ONE:
THE HUNGER YEARS

THE DEATH OF A CITY

In 1944 and 1945, long before I came home from the war, the City of Coblence, my home town, was largely destroyed by percussion and fire bombs. Beginning on April 22, 1944, in four major and many minor air raids, seven-eighths of the City was ruined.

Such, then, was my city when I returned in early 1946. Its destruction and rebuilding, like death and re-birth: they belong together and thus form a continuous story. It therefore seems right to include in it a few pictures of Coblence in peacetime and more pictures about how it died. With the armistice on May 8 came the occupation soldiers, first American and then French.

These photographs were taken from a book written by Rudolf Bauer. It is entitled: *Coblence, the Way It Was*. In the last year of the war, so says the book, life in Coblence was "one between flames and the air-raid bunker." Every tenth citizen was to die.

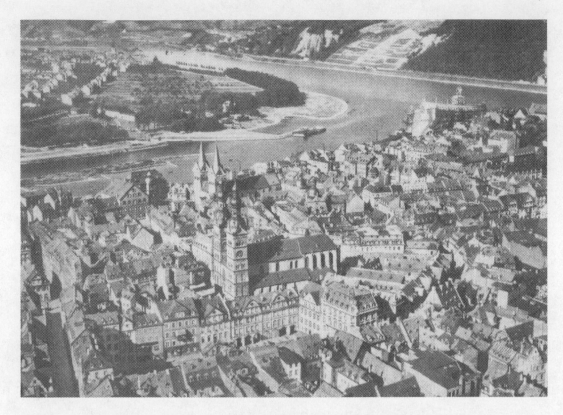

Peacetime Coblence with Churches of St. Florin (Protestant) and Our Dear Lady (Catholic)

To the hissing of steam and clanking of chains, opening the pontoon bridge between Coblence and Ehrenbreitstein

April 22, 1944

The Epicopal Castle

The stumps of the Horchheim bridge

14

Our Dear Lady   St. Florin's

Christ Church (Protestant)

Civilians leaving the City

German medical officers surrendering with Red Cross flag

American troops crossing the Rhine on a pontoon bridge

Cautiously, American troops advance into the City streets

American infantry in street fighting

American soldier standing guard near Görres Monument

American troops crossing the Moselle in boats

and hoisting the Stars and Stripes on Ehrenbreitstein Castle

French occupation troops enjoyed "pomp and circum-
stance" no less than their German predecessors

North African troops marching through town

HOME AT LAST

To the very end of the war Father had been an obedient soldier and loyal follower of Adolf Hitler. On February 2, 1944, still believing in victory he had written to Mother from windswept and wintry Ukraine: "Gerhard will not stay any longer in the USA than necessary" -- as if I would be given a choice. "Like me, you surely long for the day when we can pick him up at the ship, so that he may take root in his beautiful *Heimat* ..." (an all-encompassing German word, without equivalent in English: home, "roots," native region, Fatherland).

Well, on January 30, 1946 -- thirteen years to the day after Hitler's ascension to power -- Father and I, discharged POWs, were reunited with Mother and Cousins Hans and Marguerite Dietz at the badly bombed railroad station in Weilburg, some forty miles east of Coblence. We hiked across the Lahn bridge, up the hill and through the dimly lit town with its narrow houses and crooked streets. Bombed out in Coblence two years earlier, Mother had been assigned a small apartment next to the manse where Pastor Hans Dietz and his sister resided.

Our back-yard apartment had a small kitchen, a living room with a couch, a tiny bathroom and a mid-size bedroom. It was warm. Mother had prepared a simple dinner, for food was scarce. It was good to be home, no matter how small that home or simple that meal.

The main part of our house was occupied by a family from Saxony. Their apartment had probably been requisitioned by the American authorities and given to one of the German scientists who had been spirited away from the advancing Russians to get to the United States and, eventually, to work on ballistic missiles and other sophisticated weaponry useful in a cold war just then beginning. There were a couple of dozen such scientists in Weilburg.

The first night, and for several weeks to come, I slept on the living-room couch. After a late evening of talk, catching up on people and events, I slept soundly, as a good soldier would. But I got up early. In fact, Father and Mother were still "sleeping in." I remember being a little irritated at that. Father was 55, Mother 52; and they had not slept together for almost two years. Parents are not so different from other couples, after all.

In vain, Father and Mother had searched for news from Fritz, missing in Russia since 1943. Richard, a sprouting medical doctor, was working in an "Ami" hospital in nearby Wetzlar. Soon, he came to visit briefly. He was his usual energetic and boisterous self and told tall stories of his leaving a POW camp in the British Zone on the company sergeant's bicycle and of his present work as a medical orderly -- stories less than flattering to his American superiors. Still, he had a place to sleep and "Ami" food.

Already, "Ami" was the standard half-ridiculing, half-admiring term for these noisy and strapping uniformed guys frequenting the streets of Weilburg. The "Amis" seemed to own town, from their casern further up the hill, some of the nicest houses on Frankfurtherstrasse and their own rough-ridden trucks and jeeps.

First exploratory walks into town confirmed the strange dissonance between occupiers, swaggering, and the occupied, beset. Perhaps the contrast was the sharper for the damp and dreary weather and the quaint, pretty setting of Weilburg, a medieval charmer on its perch in a loop of the Lahn River, dominated by a sprawling Renaissance castle.

The Germans' spirits were subdued, their attitudes sullen and their stomachs empty. Nine months after the crushing and devastating defeat they were visibly preoccupied with the bare necessities of life: a loaf of bread, a warm coat, a bag of potatoes or coal, a place to stay, a bed to sleep in. Only from the passing train and some distance had I as yet seen the destruction and misery of a larger city; and Weilburg was largely intact.

Uncle Hans (Ha) and Aunt Marguerite (Ma), his sister, were as kind and welcoming as ever. Uncle Ha had at least some access to flour, potatoes and meat, what with several farm villages in his large parish. He advised Father and me about first steps as civilians: registration with the police, always mandatory in Germany; where to get ration cards; how to gain access to my dormant bank account.

Each person, in the form of coupons, was entitled to so many pounds a month of potatoes, loaves of bread, quarter-pounds of margarine, quarts of milk and half-pounds of meat or cold cuts. The food coupons were in quantities ranging from hardly to barely enough for a grown man. Both Father and I weighed less than 110 pounds; and we received extra rations of milk and "fat" the first month. After Attichy, another and much longer hungry stretch lay ahead, we knew, with no improvement in sight.

Except for rationed food, quite inexpensive, nothing could be bought -- albeit at forbidding prices on the black market. Even though I had accumulated more than 10,000 *Reichsmark* on a meager lieutenant's salary of about 250 *Mark* a month ($60), money was not just worthless but useless. A pack of cigarettes on the black market ran as much as 200 *Mark*, about the same as a pair of nylon stockings. These two were the main "currencies." Only farmers, butchers, black marketeers and men and women -- especially women -- "in" with the "Amis" were prospering. But they were a small minority in the population. Most people worried, labored and scrounged day-in, day-out to eke out a living, less by money than by services, barter and wit.

My own material possessions had reached home with me in that "Ami" duffel bag, stripped of only a few valuables on the "frisking meadow" in Attichy. A warm pair of GI slacks, dyed navy-blue and beginning to be threadbare; a smart-looking field jacket, also dyed blue; a heavy GI coat of like color, reaching to my thighs; some underwear, including a pair of longjohns; and half a dozen heavy socks whose feet were of many colors and threads from years of clumsy darning: such were my earthly possessions.

No, not quite so. There were the left-overs of my aborted military career: the breeches with that leather-seat, never mind my inability to become an officer horseman earlier; my Africa-uniform jacket and shirt; and, yes, those ill-fitting officers' boots which the guards should have taken away from me in Attichy! Years later, under circumstances shrouded in mystery but perhaps through a swift act on Heidi's part, both boots and breeches disappeared. Good riddance!

Whether in "Ami" blue or in German "GI" wear, I did not look much different from many other ex-soldiers who had to make do with little more than what they wore on their backs. So what: I was young and getting stronger by the day. And I was home, alive and unharmed -- unlike so many. Later, I would find out that of the eight who had graduated with me from high school in January 1939, only three were still alive.

I was twenty-four. It was time to move forward. It was time to go to school again, after a seven-year "interlude." To which university should I apply; in which line of study? Trains were barely running, and it was difficult to get to the nearest universities: Mainz, Frankfurt, Darmstadt, Giessen, Marburg.

Application forms were filled out diligently. All of them probed my political past. Would my having been a company commander in the pre-Hitler Youth *Jungvolk* thwart my entry into the halls of higher learning? Perhaps. But then there must have been thousands of soldiers coming home and wanting to study; and I had not been a member of the Party.

The process of denazification was just beginning, the American occupation authorities pushing it vigorously. I worked my way through a long questionnaire secured from the city government. Even then, I was struck by the notion that the "Amis" believed in both the process and the veracity of questionnaires when I knew perfectly well that some of the most virulent Nazis had been cautious enough never to sign up for Party membership. Many other "mild" types, for reasons of professional advancement or "innocent patriotism," had done so. Still, I was uncertain and even troubled a bit about how my case would be treated by Germans and Americans alike who had to sort out the "bad apples" in a very large barrel indeed!

The verdict came within a few weeks: my "affiliation" was forgiven because of my youthful age. I was relieved: my chances for entering university had been greatly enhanced. My three semesters as a POW correspondence student at the University of Minnesota were a plus, too.

In his denazification process Father could hardly claim "youthful innocence." I am no longer sure whether he went through his purge in Weilburg or Coblence, where he returned to in the spring of 1946 to resume his pastoral duties. Having been a Party member since early 1934 and a company commander in the National Socialist Motor Vehicle Corps, he was found a *Mitläufer*, literally one who had gone along with the ways of the Party. At that relatively mild verdict he may have been relieved, although he never spoke of such important matters as personal responsibility, guilt and expiation.

However, long after he had re-established himself as a hard-working and prominent pastor in Coblence, with his own Sunday morning worship broadcast -- radio being a new medium for such religious expressions -- he ran afoul of a French colonel who remained adamant in his insistence that Father "shall not preach in the Cathedral" (St. Florin's Church). In spite of support, albeit lukewarm, from the representative of the Church of the Rhineland in the French Zone, *Kirchenrat* Sachsse, Father was transferred to the Protestant parish in Engers, a medieval and pretty town twelve miles down the Rhine River. By that time in 1949 he was almost sixty. So much about denazification. Back to 1946.

My first trip brought me to Coblence, Mainz, Worms, Darmstadt and Frankfurt. It was dismal. The direct railroad line between Weilburg and Coblence was out; several bridges were still down. A circuitous line ran through the Westerwald hill country. Already, it was difficult to get from one occupation zone to another. Several seemingly harmless travelers were taken off the train. But my discharge papers, identifying me as a former resident of Coblence, got me through -- after a few minutes of apprehension.

On that winter day of 1946 the City of Coblence bore little resemblance to the thriving, beautiful and history-laden capital of the Rhineland in 1939. Eighty-seven percent of the city was destroyed. There was hardly a house undamaged. All bridges were out. Ferries provided faltering service. A few streetcars were running in the inner city, as were a few trains.

Kaiser Friedrich Strasse, that lovely tree-lined "allée," had been renamed to innocuous "Südallee," to be done with Prussian history for good. Most of the stately sycamore trees had been destroyed or felled for firewood. The tennis courts across the street were a disheveled field of weeds and bomb craters.

Our impressive four-story city house had collapsed, the concrete floors having slipped into a huge bomb crater where the gate to the unkempt lot between it and the Hilda Girls' High School had once been the goal for hot "tennis-ball soccer" matches. But, I found out later, Mother, with the help of some soldiers assigned by Father, had saved most of the family treasures: Chinese vases, Japanese jewelry, photographs, exquisite porcelain and silver utensils.

Coblence, my once fine city, was cold and desolate, almost a stranger, on that first visit. Its destruction and misery, if further evidence were needed, were stark proof that the war was lost and that normal life, with enough food and shelter, would be long in returning. I took one of the handful of trains along the Rhine to Mainz, badly damaged, and on to Worms to visit the parents of Kurt, my last driver in North Africa.

Kurt Weil's parents were gracious hosts for a day in history-rich but disfigured Worms. They owned a brewery and thus had some access to food and culture comforts. Kurt, separated from me in our first POW camp in Tunisia, run by vengeful French troops, had been made to stay in North Africa. Although mail censoring revealed little of his circumstances, he was doing "hard labor" on some railroad line going south into the high plateaus of Algeria. He -- and many like him -- had a bad time of it and did not come home until a couple of years later.

A ferry took me across the Rhine. The railroad bridge had been blown up in the last weeks of the war: the once solid piers were but stumps of stone; the girders, steel twisted at odd angles. It was a frosty and unfriendly day. Soon, the train on the local line chugged through the frozen countryside in the direction of Darmstadt. The train was drafty. All windows were out. Someone had emptied his bowels not far from my dilapidated seat.

But then, in Lorsch, two very pretty girls in their late teens, bundled up against the cold, entered the coach, navigated around that smelly pile and sat down across the aisle. Anxious to get to know them, I soon fell into an animated conversation with them, surely trying to impress. They listened and talked and laughed with ease, the two sisters, Katharina and Elisabeth. They were like the promise of spring on a miserable day, and of the attraction and love women might offer a man after his POW years of solitude. Our ways parted in Darmstadt, where I turned in my application at the *Technische Hochschule*, a university for engineering and other technical professions.

Around the end of March I was accepted at the Phillips University in Marburg, classes to start within a month. Before World War I Father had studied theology in Marburg. All I knew about it was that it was an old city of some 25,000 people; and that it had played a part in the Reformation when Luther, having broken with the Catholic Church, gradually became beholden to Protestant princes; among them Phillip of Hesse who badly wanted a divorce, which the great Reformer was persuaded to sanction.

Before I get to the diligent if hungry pursuit of my studies in Marburg and my small assigned room with the Communist Party village chairman in Cappel, an hour's hike away, I need to report on my return to the soccer field. With spring coming, the Weilburg *Sportverein* offered not only my favorite pastime but possible food. More about that angle later, for food was the greatest need, perhaps even more than women!

Soccer came in the form of a small, agile and slightly shifty dance-studio owner and soccer-club president by the name of Heini Röcken. During the war years dancing had been forbidden. While food and other comforts were badly lacking, dancing seemed like the right kind of fun, indeed of normalcy returning. And so, with soccer came dancing, an important and coveted skill which my war years in distant places had prevented me from acquiring.

Although musical -- I thought -- I had a hard time of it; and especially with the three-quarter beat of waltzes and polkas. Still and as always, I applied myself. It felt good to hold a young woman in one's arms, even if the feet were not yet in harmony. After two dozen lessons I became reasonably surefooted. With tennis and soccer, dancing became my favorite "sport."

When I registered an interest in playing soccer and to my dismay, the coach and senior player on the first team, a pleasant fellow and policeman who had played for the first-league Frankfurt *Sportverein*, had me play a trial match on the second team. I did all right and for the next two years or so I played for the S. V. Weilburg, as right or left center forward and eventually its captain.

Soon, the matches moved from the gravelly and uneven field in the casern, where our efforts were considered "weird" by the "Amis," to one near the Lahn River. It was less than square and prone to being flooded, but its surface was level and just right. We played in the county league. Several players are remembered and should enliven these pages.

The goalie came from a dirt-poor family, was married and gathering an early crop of kids. He was into spectacular saves, but his positioning in the 16-meter box was suspect. Once early on, he suffered a strange calamity. Under his padded shorts he must have worn some underpants. They were held in place, he explained afterwards, by a string -- which broke. So here was our goalkeeper poking around in his pants in the middle of the game to "get ahold of himself" without conceding a goal!

Willi Heinen was the left defender. He was a hefty guy and as a soldier had last served as orderly to Field Marshal Kesselring in Italy. Stories about that distinction were usually introduced by "I and the Field Marshal!" Willi was a butcher who had found refuge in Weilburg after being bombed out in a city in the lower Rhineland. He grew relatively stout and slow soon. He and his outgoing Rhenish wife measured my meager meat and sausage rations with solicitous generosity.

The captain, playing the "sweeper," was a scrappy former air-force officer decorated with the Knight's Cross -- not that that mattered on the soccer field. Up front, outside left, played a young and hungry-looking fellow with a nimble left foot and deft dribbles. A year later he would be killed in a strange accident: a big container being hoisted by a crane came loose and crushed him. Our point man was a real goal-getter. Heinz, a policeman too, was as unpredictable as he was dangerous.

Two other players, altogether different in looks, age and skill levels, were especially close to me. Karl Henss, the coach, was in his mid-thirties and slowing down a bit as an inside left or right forward. He and I formed the same kind of soccer symbiosis that I had enjoyed with Laafs of the Cologne Sportsclub '98 in Crossville, Tennessee. Karl, like Laafs, was a much better player than I, a professional with all the tricks in the book and elegant passes; and I was his necessary, rangy and inexhaustible helpmate ever bent on moving the attack forward from mid-field.

Abbie was not his real name. He was a handsome, lithe and happy-go-lucky fellow of about nineteen, a baker's apprentice and sprouting ladies' man. He may have seen in me an older and battle-tried model, both on the soccer field and, soon, on the dance floor. We became best friends.

In one of the first matches on the new soccer field we played against Karl Henss' former club. A crowd of several hundred cheered us on -- to an odd 5:5 draw. I had an especially good day as outside-right attacker, with sheer luck for spinning corner kicks and lobs, and one goal. Afterwards Karl told me of an offer for me to play for the Frankfurt *Sportverein*. It was an honor easily declined.

Within a year our eleven played in the regional league, which included teams from the "big" cities of Giessen, Marburg and Wetzlar. We finished a respectable fourth in 1948. I am getting ahead, though, of my soccer-*cum*-study story and of commuting between my barren room in Cappel and the soccer-and-dance weekends in Weilburg, a distance of some forty miles.

That "social life" was rich and exciting. Clearly, I tried to make up for lost time. There was the last Weilburg commandant's daughter, a pretty and buxom girl and a superb waltz dancer. There was Elfriede, less than pretty but with a good figure -- and an avid soccer fan. There were others, their names forgotten. It was good to fondle and kiss and conquer. Dancing was the overture to all that.

The Weilburger Hof was the principal attraction in this regard: a live band, watery beer -- only the "Amis" had the regular stuff -- a restless young crowd. I was probably among the older ones, after seven years in the war. The girls seemed to like me, or so I thought.

The parents having moved back to Coblence, I did not have a room in Weilburg. Enter *Herr* Schnupp, the fat, sleezy, short and shifty owner of a café where he also rented out rooms. To call his place a hotel would be a considerable exaggeration. He was "in" with the "Amis" for whom he baked and who, in turn, provided him with flour, *Starkbier* (real beer) and other goodies; and who, all too easily, prevailed upon him to rent a few rooms for the GIs' one-night stands -- for more goodies. Schnupp knew how to make the best of otherwise lousy times. And so Schnupp's café, a small room under the gabled roof and an often unmade bed became my weekend lodging. Of course, *Herr* Schnupp was also an enthusiastic soccer fan.

A block away from Schnupp's in the Hotel zur Krone, off-limits for German men, the "Amis" held forth. For us, too, there was no longer a curfew. But when the band at the Weilburger Hof stopped playing at midnight, there was still a lot of raucous noise and bawdy laughter at the Krone; and clusters of German women with heavy makeup and solicitous ways. From the big band inside music spilled onto the street: to our ears, the somewhat jarring cadences of "In the Mood." And yet, most of us liked the new and alien beat.

For us, often hungry and sipping watery beer, there was some envy of those who had enough food, comfort and *Starkbier*. The world seemed to be sharply and unfairly divided between that of us have-nots and theirs of haves. In our hearts both envy and dislike were strangely mixed.

In general, "Ami" girls were shunned and maligned by much of the German populace, young and old. As it was, the "Amis" lived in their own ghettos, surrounded by a small army of "camp followers."

During the summer break of 1946 I paid a sentimental visit to Wiedenest, the age-old village where I was born and raised. I stayed at the half-timbered house of one branch of the widespread Köster clan. For once, food was ample.

In its appearance the village was unchanged, its ways solid, its looks pretty. But every house was full to the rafters with refugees from the east, their presence grudgingly tolerated by the natives. Hans Zimmermann had been shot down over Sicily in 1943. His older brother Kurt had joined the S. S. and was still in some POW camp. Erika Sauerteig, playmate when we were not yet in school, had married her father's apprentice and was helping her never-stand-still mother. Bo, the trout-fisher, always poor and often hungry, had died a soldier's death, too. Two of the Mesenhöhler girls, now in their early twenties, were still unmarried and, to my delight, full of young love.

Busy with my studies in Marburg and the weekends in Weilburg, I yet pursued an active correspondence with former friends and fellow POWs. Meinhart, my best friend from the high-school days in Coblence, who had fled to England just in time, had changed his name from Meinhart Katz to Michael Heathcote, was a teacher, married and had two children. Quite understandably, he was virulently anti-German. Our correspondence did not last long.

I wrote to Mr. Myers, the principal of the Simon Langton Boys' School in Canterbury. But he never replied. Fellow POW Arthur, though, did. He had married his Dutch sweetheart Reemda. I visited the Wittes in their nice apartment in Friesland where I wrote the prologue to this story. Loga is near the North Sea shore. I even took a trip to Borkum; but the pre-war ambiance of that island, with its middle-class vacationers, refined ways and Continental music on the wide boardwalk, was gone. Borkum was but an empty shell of its once charming life. A few blown-up bunkers were a quiet reminder that here, too, the war seemed to have put a dismal and irrevocable end to my cherished childhood memories.

It must have been in the summer of 1946 that I visited the Wittmers in Hagen, a large and grimy factory city in the Ruhr valley. "Father" Wittmer was a dentist and therefore not without food and other enjoyable wherewithal. Earlier that year Richard had fallen in love with the elder Wittmer daughter, Gerda, a bit older than he; pretty, blue-eyed, with blond hair and an aqualine nose -- and noticeably pregnant. This turn of events dismayed both the Wittmers and our parents. Still, they were gracious hosts. Father conducted the church wedding ceremony in the fall. In January 1947, a daughter was born, Regina -- destined to take to very radical causes in the sixties but not to marriage.

Richard had been accepted at the Goethe University in Frankfurt, four war-time semesters to his credit. He and Gerda had found a small apartment in Frankfurt-Sindlingen. I remember a pleasant visit with them. Gerda had baked a fake *Kuchen* -- from a bit of flour and milk, "fat" and, mostly, wheat flakes. For Richard and his expectant wife-to-be, as for me, these were very lean student years.

In and around the Frankfurt-Höchst railroad station, not far from the desolate and much maligned Höchst Farbenwerke, stretching along the tracks for a mile, there loitered and lurked dozens of Jewish black-marketeers from the nearby Zeilsheim Displaced Persons' camp. Having nothing to offer, I watched them do brisk business with American soldiers and some German civilians. My curiosity was not entirely without envy. Yet this was not my world, hungry or not.

During the summer months of 1946 I seriously entertained the thought of joining the French Foreign Legion. My military training and natural discipline might have served me well. I had heard or read somewhere that many former German soldiers were doing so, surely not for *l'Amour de la Patrie* but for a secure, if tough, life with a roof over one's head and a meal in one's stomach. But I lacked the courage for such an extraordinary "career."

One of the reasons for dreaming of a better life was the growing disenchantment with my studies in Marburg. In my second semester in the harsh "potato winter" of 1946-47, when even potatoes were scarce, I took essentially the same courses, had the same teachers and hiked three-quarter hours every day to the Marburg-Süd railroad station, from where the one tramline through the city was running regularly. And back at nightfall to my often cold room with the Groebs.

I had added Dr. von Rauch to my handful ot teachers. He taught a course on "Swedish dominance in the Baltic." A hundred or more students crowded his lectures. They were superb: lucid and full of interesting detail; and war-mongering, albeit heroic, rulers like Gustavus Adolphus and Charles XII. Dr. von Rauch's contagious teaching was regularly rewarded with a thunderous stomping of the feet, a new and strange behavior for this attentive and appreciative student.

My small room on the second floor of the Groebs' relatively new house was not bad at all. My landlords, however, were far less likable, although *Frau* Groeb offered me a bowl of soup or a chunk of bread now and then. In her early forties and plain, she was the best of the lot, by far. *Herr* Groeb, a mason by trade, a slight, surly and seamy man with slick hair, was a full-fledged black-marketeer. His two lean and mean teenage sons were junior partners in the thriving business. They smoked and drank some of the stuff they traded. As the chairman of the local Communist

Party chapter, *Herr* Groeb was unassailable in his little empire. I would not have put it past him to keep a little record of the behavior of former small-time Nazis in the village!

And then there was the seven-year old daughter, a measly and wicked thing: noisy and nosy, insatiable in her curiosity about me and, worse, my meager belongings. Still, Cappel was an undamaged and peaceful farmers' village. On occasion, I would see women carry boards with large round loaves of bread to be baked in the communal oven. Worse than seeing was to inhale the marvelous scent of fresh-baked bread, so far beyond my reach.

It was exceedingly difficult to visit my parents in Coblence in the French Zone. Nevertheless, I saw them a couple of times in the summer and fall of 1946. They lived in a large turn-of-the-century house on Metternicher Strasse, a good two miles from the center of Coblence. All four Moselle bridges were still out, and there were no trams or buses going to and from Metternich.

The parents lived on the ground floor. A mother and daughter, also bombed out, lived on the second floor. The parish deaconess, Sister Anna, an elderly and dour woman, lived in the attic. With millions of refugees from the German provinces turned over to Poland under the Yalta agreements, as well as bombed-out persons in the three western occupation zones, all living space was assigned by the German *Wohnungsamt*, under the tall authority of occupation officials who had priority claims.

The parents' furniture was simple -- mostly pieces donated by more fortunate parish members. A lean-on to the house had a laundry kitchen; and there was a sturdy washer woman. She came every two weeks and relieved Mother of the heavy chore of heating water in big kettles, rubbing the laundry on washboards with smelly bars of soap, rinsing it out and hanging it on lines in the garden.

Ah, the garden.

It measured about 150 by 300 feet. From a wall in the rear one looked down upon the winding Moselle River and, to the left, see the ruined city and destroyed bridges. Stolid Fortress Ehrenbreitstein on the other side of the Rhine gazed down upon the confluence of the two rivers and the desolate city.

The vegetables and fruits of the garden became lifesavers, literally. Pears, apples, plums and peaches abounded, as did carrots, tomatoes, radishes, lettuce, peas and beans. Hard-working and less than robust,

Father made time and found strength to increase the harvest, what with the excellent pumicestone-rich soil. A little family joke applies. Mother might say to her husband: "Fritz, watch the third rung on the old stepladder!" It meant that he was to go into the garden and fetch a load of apples or pears! That fall of 1946, in the large living room reserved for official but non-existent parish business, hundreds of apples and pears were spread out on the floor, filling the room with a delicious fruity scent. I will return to that scent in a bit.

Old friends in Wiedenest had helped me find the children of grade-school teacher Otto Degenhard, that stern and superb schoolman. Remember: his wife had died in childbirth when little Hilde was born in 1937; and *Herr* Degenhard, no longer young, volunteered for military service in Russia, where he was killed. My saved money was mostly useless. Perhaps out of gratitude for the "old man" or pity for his orphaned children, I felt that I should help them. From the summer of 1946 to the currency reform in June 1948, I kept sending fifty *Reichsmark* to their grandparents every month.

Of greater consequence was meeting Hildegard Schrader during one of my visits in Coblence. Mother more than Father, perhaps hoping to "fix me up" witih someone pretty, nice and respectable -- especially respectable -- had suggested that I call on her at the Markenbildchenweg pharmacy. Without enthusiasm, I did.

Hilde, in her white uniform, was exceptionally attractive: a youthful figure, most regular facial features with blue eyes and dark-blond hair combed back. Even more striking was her cool poise. Whenever I was in Coblence during the next year we would spend time together: just walking through the rubble-seamed streets or along the Rhine, talking; even in her small room at a convent on Entenpfuhl in the oldest part ot the city where she had found shelter and the protection of friendly but strict nuns.

We grew quite fond of each other. My mail register in that small war-paper handmade booklet still in my possession shows that I wrote her regularly. In that same *Notizbuch* is an account of our relationship in that dreary November of 1946. It is called *Ein Spaziergang* -- a walk.

The weather was cold and wet. Fog and rain showers engulfed the destroyed city. The ice on the pools along the Moselle was a dirty-gray sheet. Long since, my feet were wet.

We sat in your room. It was small. Yet some ornaments brought Christmas near. Our conversation was faltering, a so often in recent months. The apple you offered and the tiny *Schnapps* could not overcome our inability, in feelings and words, to come closer to each other. Nor could the Christmas cookies; or the play of your slender fingers on that antique spinning wheel.

You suggested a walk to end the awkward silence. We walked through gray streets. The dead and crumbled façades of houses caught the fog and drizzle. The only sounds were our swishing steps and the rain dripping from roofs, trees and ruins.

I must have proposed that we go our separate ways; meaning, quietly and without struggle -- each one into the cold, wet, gray and hungry workday. Perhaps one day we might find, miraculously, a radiant happiness. I must have said, later on: "It's a pity. It would have been so good to understand each other with a little love and joy."

I notice, stealthily from the corner of my eye, how tears seem to well up in your eyes. A long silence. And I see your face: the steep forehead, the straight finely chiseled nose and the slightly open mouth with just a hint of trembling. I would love to kiss that mouth, again and again, and hug you firmly and long. Are you waiting for that? I do not know and do not have the courage for it.

"If you care to" -- she uses the formal *Sie* -- "you may write," before she offers me a slender and cool hand to say good-bye. For good? I do not know and dare not ask.

Hilde was so different from the girls I danced and went out with in Weilburg, so reserved, so much of a lady. She was not for amorous pursuit, not one for playing. She was for loving, caring, trusting -- and marrying. Was I ready for that? No, I was not. She may not have been either.

Tram lines ran only in the inner city. For Father and me, walking was the ticket. He spent hours every day just covering the considerable distances to the parish office on Mainzerstrasse and to suburban gathering places for Bible School and intermittent church services; as well as calling on the sick, dying and distraught. Father deeply cared for his parishioners, one on one, especially since the post-war climate with its return to religion favored an active worship and parish life.

But just as he had not shared his deeper feelings and possible conflicts in the years of our adolescence, when he found himself on contested "neutral" ground in a parish polarized between German Christians, pro-Hitler, and members of the Confessing Church, anti-Hitler, so now he did not reveal his emotions and struggles to "make good."

He knew full well that some of his long-time parishioners had not forgotten his active role in the National Socialist Party. Although he had always denied membership as a German Christian, an article I came across recently mentioned Father's name as such. For all the contretemps then and now, for possible scruples then and now, Father stuck indefatigably to his preaching, visiting and administering.

As for Mother, after her early espousal of National Socialism and probable later disenchantment, heightened by Fritz' death, she was busy getting enough food on the table and clothing on our backs. Now and then circumstances forced her to take the train into the fertile fields and fat villages of the nearby Eifel hills to pick leftover potatoes or apples or scrounge for other foodstuffs. She did not complain. She also did not share her deeper feelings or political views with us -- when the rough treatment of the populace by the French and the tentative efforts of politicians "left over" from the Weimar Republic were certainly inviting discussion topics.

Or, for that matter, her and Father's responsibility for Hitler's rise to power and its devastating and now incriminating consequences. Shame, guilt and the desire for expiation for the recent past may well have been there; and the possible blame, expressed by many of the short-memoried, for the Allies -- the Russians more than those of the West. Though present in the parents' minds and hearts, aired and discussed they were not. And I doubt that they were between Father and Mother.

During the winter of 1946-47 I landed my first major post-war acquisition: a used bicycle. For the hefty sum of 800 *Reichsmark* a black marketeer in the city was willing to part with it. Father used the bike when I was not in Coblence.

LITERARY INTERESTS

Inspired by Dr. Schneider's demanding classes, I entered what might be called a literary phase. I read several English novels. In fact, I copied excerpts from a few cherished ones in my little gray notebook. Fifty years later I marvel at my small and neat handwriting when, in the last fifteen years, I have shifted to printed letters. Here are two, from John Galsworthy's *The Island Pharisees*, of course referring to the British.

Each man born into the world is born to go a journey, and for the most part he is born on the high road. At first he sits there in the dust, with his little chubby hands reaching at nothing, and his little solemn eyes staring into space. As soon as he can toddle, he moves, by the queer instinct we call love of life, straight along this road, looking neither to the right nor the left, so pleased is he to walk. And he is charmed with everything -- with the nice flat road, all broad and white, with his own feet, and with the prospect he can see on either side.

The sun shines and he finds the road a little hot and dusty; the rain falls and he splashes through the muddy puddles. It makes no matter -- all is pleasant; his father went this way before him; they made this road for him to tread, and, when they bred him, passed into his fibre the love of doing things as they themselves had done them. So he walks on and on, resting comfortably at night under the roofs that have been raised to shelter him, by those who went before.

Suddenly, one day, without intending to, he notices a path or opening in the hedge leading to left or right, and he stands still, looking at the undiscovered. After that he stops at all openings in the hedge. One day, with a beating heart, he tries one. And this is where the fun begins.

But of ten of him that try the narrow path, nine come back to the broad road and, when they pass the next gap in the hedge, they say: "No, no, my friend, I found you pleasant for a while, but after that -- ah, after that! The way my fathers went is good enough for me, and it is obviously the proper one; for nine of me came back, and that poor silly tenth -- I really pity him!"

And when he comes to the next inn, and snuggles in his well-warmed bed, he thinks of the wild waste of heather where he might have had to spend the night beneath the stars, nor does it occur to him that the broad road he treads was once a trackless heath itself.

But the poor silly tenth is faring on. It is a windy night that he is travelling through -- a windy night with all things new around, and nothing to help him but his courage. Nine times out of ten that courage fails, and he goes down in the bog. He has seen the undiscovered, and the undiscovered has engulfed him; his spirit, tougher than the spirit of the nine that hurried back to sleep in inns, was not yet tough enough. The tenth time he wins across, and on the traces he has left others follow slowly, cautiously -- and a new road is opened to mankind.

Another excerpt from *The Island Pharisees* talks about mankind being divided into classes. A later notation in my notebook gives a German version of the same theme: "They drank mocha, not coffee, like some common people!"

Everything seemed divided into classes, carefully docketed and valued. For instance, a Briton was of more value than a man, and wives than women. -- They do you awfully well, he said. A voice from a chair on Shelton's (he is the hero of the story) right replied: They do you better at Verado's. The Veau d'Or's the best place: They give you Turkish baths for nothing! The suavity of this pronouncement engulfed all as with a blessing. And at once, as if by magic, in the oak-paneled room, the world fell naturally into its three departments: that where they do you well; that where they do you better; and that where they give you Turkish baths for nothing.

If you want Turkish baths, said a tall youth with a clean red face, you should go, you know, to Budapest, most awfully rippin' there. Oh no, said the man perched on the fender: A Johnny I know tells me they are nothing compared to Sofia. His face was transfigured by the subtle gloating of a man enjoying vice by proxy. Ah, drawled the small-mouthed man: There is nothing fit to hold a candle to Baghdad. Once again his utterance enfolded all as with a blessing; and once again the world fell into its three departments: that where they do you well; that where they do you better; and -- Baghdad!

The little gray notebook shifts to German, to a short poem particularly fitting for our war generation and the first hard years after the war.

Possessions lost, something lost!
Must move with spin
New ones to win.

Honor lost, much is lost!
Must win new glory,
And people will tell your story.

Courage lost, all is lost!
Your very life would be the cost.

My notebook was becoming a memory bank: of letters written, of friendships made, renewed or lost; of impressions, good and bad; of things read and found worthwhile. It was a time when, still subconsciously, I began to adopt English as my favorite language: malleable, moving with its verbs, not standing stiffly at attention with its nouns like German; English, a language like a water-color drawing, not the oil painting of French or Spanish. Still, I was far from mastering it. English is a most difficult language.

There was an excerpt from Rilke's *Cornet*, the story of a young nobleman in the Austrian wars against the Turks, who died far away from home and all too early.

To rest. For once, to be a guest. Not always to satisfy your wishes with meager meals. Not always to grasp for everything in hostile ways. Just for once, to let things happen to you, knowing what happens is good. Courage, too, must just for once surrender and roll over along the seams of silken sheets. Not always, to be a soldier. Just for once, to let your hair fall down in long curls, to open your collar wide and to sit on a damask armchair; and to feel to your very fingertips like after a marvelous bath.

And to learn again what women are like. How the white ones do, and the blue ones; what hands they have; and how they sing their laughter when blond boys bring in handsome bowls, brimful with juicy fruits.

There are little essays about the signs of the hard times: a concert in a cold church, the city auditorium still a pile of rubble -- a first sign of a civil and cultured society coming back to its senses and feelings; a "meeting with the Roman Catholic Church," when I delivered a congratulatory message from Father to Monsignor Homscheid on his 25th anniversary as a priest. Said he before bidding me good-bye: "Well, well, 13 degrees tonight. When I started my ministry 25 years ago, it was 10 degrees." Did he say, twenty-five years? It seemed to me that he said "Nineteen-hundred." As timeless as his Church, so was he, the Monsignor.

And there was an odd assortment of "thought splinters":

Comradeship was the cathedral of our lives, friendship the altar, the war our yearning: I do not know what could have shaken our fortitude.

He belonged to that group of people who could sit in the little box of their own heart, like a miniature Chinese god, legs folded under, always doubting, and even smiling about, himself.

(From Binding's *Remembrances*) How many kisses remain unkissed because no other lips are near; how many tears unshed because there is no one with whom one could cry. And so kisses fall on lips which happen to be near, and flowers cry because someone is near with whom they can cry. But each one believes that the near lips blossom, and each tear is shed, only for him.

POLITICS

If 1946-47 witnessed the stirring of my literary and even poetic soul, these years also saw the awakening of my political interest. Like many of my war-time vintage, in which every second man did not make it home, I attached ardent hopes to a new and democratic Germany rising from the ashes of destruction and the embers of patriotism all but extinguished. Such hope was not easy to come by.

The Fatherland had become a much smaller and more crowded place. The victors at Yalta, to reward the Soviet Union for its immense losses in human life and treasure, and for its decisive role in winning the war, had given half of East Prussia and all of Pomerania and Silesia to Poland -- to compensate the latter, in turn, for the loss of its eastern third to Russia. Millions of refugees, fleeing from advancing Russian tanks and imagined Polish revenge, were crowding attics, cellars, schools and barns in the three western occupation zones.

With headquarters in East Berlin, the Russian occupation zone extended from the Oder-Neisse Line as far west as the Elbe River. It included Thuringia, Saxony, Brandenburg, Mecklenburg and Anterior Pomerania to the exclusion of Stettin. The northern part of East Prussia became a forbidden part of Russia itself, while Berlin had become a four-sector city far in the hinterland of the Russian Zone.

To a keen observer like myself, however preoccupied he may have been with his daily wherewithal, the British seemed to be the most "civilized" in their occupational behavior. The northwestern corner of the country was theirs to "rule," as well as the same corner of Berlin. Seasoned by centuries of colonial rule, they appeared to take their responsibilities naturally and seriously, but without malice.

The Americans showed their strong presence in Hesse, the enclave of Bremerhaven on the North Sea, half of Baden and all of Württemberg and Bavaria. To this very day, most Americans, informed by their then occupation and, later, "partner" troops, think of Germany as speaking, acting and living the Bavarian way; and even at present most German-American events and exchanges take on that particular flavor.

The American presence in Weilburg was not atypical: the soldiers in the barracks ghetto, yet very visible and audible in town in their off-duty hours. To us probably less than objective people, it seemed as if in their governance Americans showed a Messianic tendency of righteousness issuing into a desire to turn us, "probably Nazis all," into eager democrats; and do it overnight.

On the German side a saying went around, probably taken from the time when American and British troops freed and simultaneously occupied parts of France. It thus described the difference between the two: the British don't care who owns the place; the Americans behave as if they own it! Oh well, who are earlier German occupiers to judge their successors!

Finally, the French occupied the southern part of the Rhineland, including a bridgehead on the eastern bank near Coblence, Rheinhessen, the Palatinate west of the Rhine, the Saarland and the southern reaches of Württemberg and Baden. They also held a "sliver" of Berlin -- to make that former capital a four-zone, hard-to-govern enclave. Perhaps to compensate for the ambivalent role of the French in the war or inspired by the generation-old struggle with Germany over borderlands, the French seemed to have, and show, a nasty edge.

From the requisitioning of butter to the border controls east of Coblence to the felling and hauling away of trees, especially in the Black Forest, they extracted a heavy toll in treasure and emotions. The governor of what would eventually become the State of Rhineland-Palatinate was a proven "Free Frenchman" -- the followers of Charles De Gaulle during the war -- by the name of Bois-Lambert. Quickly, the Coblence folk re-named him "*Holz*-Lambert" or "Woodsy Lambert." Some Germans wondered even whether there was a connection between his name and the stripping of wooded mountainsides!

I did not know -- and do not now -- the exact terms of the armistice signed on May 8, 1945; and they may have been little more than requiring the unconditional surrender of all German forces and war-making potential.

Nor did I know those of the Yalta agreements of February 1945; and some clauses may have been secret.

At any rate, dismantling of factories and equipment, and removal of rolling stock, went on at a good clip, most severely in the Russian zone of occupation. Much later I would learn that the enforced removal of leading scientists from Germany to both Russia and the USA was to advance military inventions, notably in the development of long-range missiles. Perhaps such were the normal spoils of war. In 1946 the Cold War was not yet, but a wariness between the western allies and the Soviet Union was already palpable.

1946 was the year of the Nuremberg war-crime trials. Hitler and Goebbels had chosen death on the pyre of flames and rubble in Berlin, a fitting finale for their notions of Teutonic *Götterdämmerung* (dusk of the gods). Himmler had taken poison when arrested a few weeks later. But two dozens of the Third Reich's leaders deemed by the Allies to be the most important and notorious in waging war and killing millions of innocent victims were to stand trial.

The picture of these haggard, haunted, deflated and unrepentant men is kept alive in frequently shown historical films -- and in the excellent full-length movie "Judgment at Nuremberg" with Spencer Tracy as the presiding U.S. judge and Maximilian Schell as counsel for the defense.

One of the accused, Robert Ley, escaped death: he took poison; as did Hermann Göring, a few days before his execution. It has never been fully explained how a lethal capsule was smuggled into his closely watched cell.

No longer sure why I did so, I recorded what some of the convicted said just before dying. Most were hanged. Several received long prison terms. Three were acquitted: Fritsche, a propagandist; Schacht, the financial mastermind behind the restoration of the German currency after the Great Inflation of 1922-23 and, subtly, the financial backing of Hitler's march to war; and von Papen, one-time chancellor and shrewd diplomat par excellence.

> Keitel, Chief of the Joint Staffs (OKW): Now, I am following my own sons. Everything for Germany. I thank you.
> Kaltenbrunner, chief of the S. S. *Sicherheitsdienst* and one of those responsible for the holocaust: I regret that in its hour of need Germany was not exclusively led by soldiers. I regret that crimes were committed. I had no part in them. Good luck, Germany!

Frank, a Party leader and Governor-General of Poland: Long live Germany eternal!

Streicher, *Gauleiter* of Franconia and publisher of *Der Stürmer* (The Storm Trooper), the viciously anti-semitic Party paper: This is my "Purim" (Jewish festival) 1946. I will go to be with God. Some day the Communists will hang you, too. Adele, my dear wife. *Heil Hitler*!

Sauckel, Party official and in charge of forced labor: May God protect my family!

Jodl: Army Chief of Staff: I salute you, my Germany!

Seyss-Inquart, Austrian Chancellor after 1938, later Governor-General of the Netherlands: I trust that this execution will be the last act in the tragedy of the Second War and a lesson as well, so that there may be peace and understanding among nations. I believe in Germany.

This macabre record may suggest an assessment of Adolf Hitler. It comes from Brother Richard who, in his memoir, took a seasoned physician's look at the *Führer*, fifty years after his violent death in Berlin.

(After recording the essential facts in Hitler's peculiar "career," Richard wrote: Let me, from the judgment of others and my own views answer the necessary questions about Hitler's human qualities.)

He was a highly intelligent person, yet remained in his inner self a petty bourgeois. Self-taught, his thinking had nihilistic tendencies; his self-esteem was disturbed. Power-hungry, ambitious, he followed his theses fanatically and ruthlessly. In part introvert and fearful and in part uncontrollably angry; a talented speaker and negotiator with great radiation and force of conviction. Altogether, he was an extraordinary personality with a badly torn "inner image" at the edge of being pathological.

My political interest was fanned by all sorts of happenings, articles and conversations, sometimes just to break the monotony of the day and the gnawing emptiness of my stomach. Of course, many and important changes in Germany and my own life occurred between 1947 and 1952; but I will tell the story of this intense interest in one ongoing chapter to provide continuity and so to explain the gradual formation of some of my lifelong attitudes and convictions.

One train of reflection was based on excerpts from the *Frankfurter Hefte*, one of the earliest monthlies to appear on newsstands. It had some bite and took first shots at the occupying powers and, after 1951, newly powerful German politicians. Most of the following excerpts date from the early fifties when a West German government had already been formed under the watchful tutelage of the Western Allies and the firm hand of the "Old Man" -- *der Alte*, Konrad Adenauer.

The Socialist (Labour Party) victory in the elections in England was the occasion for a statement by the German Minister for Economic Development that policies of austerity would be inappropriate for Germany. What for, after all? Such rationing and economizing might be all right for a victorious nation. But why should a thoroughly beaten, bombed and, moreover, divided country so tighten its belt? Professor Ehrhard's argument is more subtle, as could be expected: Germany is a developed industrial nation. Let us be clear: while Great Britain as a primitive agrarian country ...

Behind solid barricades, American personnel began digging for Göring's gilded bathtub (how obscene his taste!). The films taken by German photographers were confiscated and destroyed. But why? Is war-booty hunting still going on? If so, why without photographers?

According to a French newspaper, Baron Arnold von Rechberg reported that at the beginning of Hitler's reign he did not at all think of persecuting Jews. The industrial magnate Pietsch and the painter Ziegler had proof of this. It was Stalin who drove Hitler toward anti-semitism, solely to cause a rift with Western Allies. Whom would this surprise? It is well known that Vishinsky (Soviet Foreign Minister) designed Goebbels' speeches and (Russian) General Rokossovsky, Keitel's army deployment. It was only at Stalingrad that the National Socialists succeeded in distancing themselves from the Bolshevic model.

"Much has been dismantled in Germany, but not the Germans' big mouth." So says a Swiss newspaper. Right or wrong, from time to time it is useful to know how unpopular one is.

The former commander of an American army group, General Devers, recently expressed his enthusiasm about the rearmament of West Germany. He said that should war break out, West Germans would love to fight the Russians under American officers. "And," he added, "the Germans can fight like devils!" What does he mean: like devils? Only recently was the pact with the devil the subject of protracted proceedings at Nuremberg. And now, here comes a fresh and frolicking

American general (Christian soldier and devil's general) and expresses in image, word and wished-for reality as if nothing had happened. As if nothing had happened.

"Russia and America," answered a house painter-to-be when asked recently in his apprentice exam to name five continents. His answer was surely unfit for an apprentice but seemed to be a master piece for describing world politics.

The German efforts regarding employee participation in work-place decisions, says the *Frankfurter Allgemeine*, have drawn some unfriendly reactions in the USA. Why, don't the Germans have any more pressing concerns? That's it: we Germans do not have enough to do. We need not produce atom bombs. We need not re-educate some foreign nationals (nor even reduce them). We need not organize the United Nations; nor defend Korea or Indochina (or, for that matter, the Elbe River). We need not internationalize Jerusalem or halve it or arabicize it. All we do is to entertain idle piffle. What a silly thing for employees to participate in management: pure product of idleness!

As came out recently, Count Schwerin, the security advisor to the Chancellor, had petitioned the Allied Security Council -- without the "Old Man's" knowledge -- to permit the German production of police weapons, including small-size mortars. Why take long detours? However authoritarian Dr. Adenauer may present himself, he remains a hopeless civilian.

However, the "international association of generals" is not yet foolproof. The Allied Council refused permission: never content, these Germans! No sooner are they permitted again to shoot they want to make money from it. There must be some differences, after all. Still, we are assured by the *Neue Zeitung*, "the Western Allies are willing to contribute to the rearmament of the German police." What luck: it would have been awkward if we would have had to buy the stuff from the Soviet Union.

Under the title "Female Spies -- for Us!" the *Münchner Illustrierte* promises stories about women who served in the German spy agencies during World War II. Whom did they spy for: for us or for Hitler?

This political interest of mine -- the keener perhaps after the cataclysmic death of the Third Reich -- kept reaching back into the war years, if mostly to see whether lessons had been learned from that dark chapter. What kind of Phoenix would rise from the ashes? What politics, policies and associations would be the emerging leaders', those either in opposition to National Socialism and miraculously spared or "left over" innocuously from the Weimar Republic, like Konrad Adenauer? Would the millions of soldiers, now civilians, have a real say after their hard fall from being heroes to being nobodies or, for many foreigners, even villains?

Reaching back into the war: the fate of tens of thousands of POWs taken by the Russians. Lucky I, having been a captive in the West! In contrast, here are excerpts from an article about German POWs in Russia, from September 1947. It was entitled "Prisoners of War under the Yoke." By then the war had been over for more than two years, but it took up to ten years for some POWs to come home from Russia. Most never made it.

POWs come from all over the Donbass, that coal-rich area in Ukraine. Most work in mines.

It is impossible to describe what goes on in Pit Six underground, called the "criminals' pit" in "Pleny" (POW) language. Girls and women work here, Russian civilians, criminals and German POWs. In this pit there is incessant harassment, scolding and cursing. Everything and everyone is haunted by the devil coal, coal and coal again. Human beings count no longer; only coal. The Russian bosses want to earn money; therefore, more coal. For the sake of personal advantage, many a German POW wants to "make up for the past" and thus obtain an extra ration of soup or mush; therefore, more coal. A POW is in constant fear that he might have to appear before the political commissar on charges of insufficient output and be sent to the "bunker" (prison) for a night or two.

After a one-mile walk below ground, through mud and water, we begin to hear the monotonous beating of the "shaking trough" (to put the coal on a conveyor belt). Ahead yawns a dark tunnel, three feet high, dirty and wet. On all fours we creep into the hole, one man behind the other, over rocks, broken pit props and coal, a distance of some 500 feet. Somewhere sits "the Killer," one of the Russian bosses, striking one man with his lantern, another with his fist and still another with the handle of his pick, entirely at will and without reason and bawling incessantly: "Dawei!" (forward).

For eight, nine or ten hours we work in the tunnel, dig coal, move rocks, drive poles into the ground, set up props and bore blast-holes.

Time passes but no one knows what time it is. Finally, tiny, tossing points of light appear and come near: the next shift ... It is cold above ground; ice-cold wind and darkness all over again. That winter, for the POWs, there was no more sun, not even daylight.

It was probably in 1949 when I came across an article in the *Frankfurter Allgemeine*, written by a Rüdiger Proske: "We out of the War." Remember the times: a conquered, divided and occupied Germany, her people cleansed of National Socialism and chastised for their wicked behavior. To talk about the war or even the role of returning POWs in the new and constrained Germany was neither expected nor prudent.

There are experiences of the war branded into us which one is not accustomed to speak about nowadays, or which one refers to only in whispers when no listener seems near. We are afraid that what we lived to see during the war may be confused with war adventures, with front-line spirit, with a war-time generation, with soldiers' or veterans' organizations or with the storm troopers. For the generation which preceded ours, war meant trenches, drum-fire and dugouts; tough suffering and endurance, and holding beleaguered outposts. What we have seen has not yet been described; and it will take a while before any of us record it on paper, for we are still turning our experiences over within us. There is a sky in our mental picture, which turns purple at 30,000 feet; and there are watch dials of soft phosphorescent green in a night slashed with lightning; and gray, green or blue seas towered over by silvery clouds; the glittering yellow of deserts and the silhouettes of tanks in front of an endless steppe; and roads, roads, roads.

This is not romanticism: we do not care about romanticism. We have seen the boundless space, the unity of space on this earth. Boundlessness is something mysterious, something dangerous for us Germans because we tend to be without measure. Many of us have fallen victim to a certain immoderateness. But only he who understands boundlessness will understand bounds. We know more of bounds and moderation than is written in books. For it was we who were lost in the sky, missed on the seas and went astray on the steppes. It was we who lived through Stalingrad and fled with half-frozen legs along Russian roads; and we are the ones who were locked in the lower holds of POW ships and passed through the German

U-boat blockade; and we were parched from heat in interrogation cages in Egypt and ran the gauntlet of French resistance fighters. We therefore know today that boundlessness and bounds, just ambition and moderation, belong to each other. But where in Germany, or the rest of the world for that matter, do we find the one or the other? Remarque (World War I author) witnessed the war as a place; we witnessed it as a journey. But both of us witnessed its horror.

We learned to hate war not only for its horror. This makes us different from Remarque. Behind "our" war, and in addition to it, there were too many other factors; when in one night we had changed from "heroes of the nation" to "militarists" we did not fully understand the change because these words, the one and the other, had long ceased to concern us. We were too much wrapped up in ourselves, in the abundance of visions rising up within us against the war, to be touched by the shrill voices of unbending ideologues and zealous opportunists. What did they know of boundlessness and bounds?

When finally one of us begins to write he is likely to say much about men -- Norwegians and Greeks, French and Russians, Italians and Dutch, Arabs and Americans. He is likely to speak about love and hatred, martial fervor and magnanimity, hostility and comradeship, of the things essential that divide and those that unite; and of the fact that in our own very need and across all fronts we often found our way to one another. The "master race" trod the roads behind us. We had no share in it. We got on well with our hosts in southern France and with the guards of our camps in the Canadian prairies. They and all others whom we met had their strong points for which we like them. They had weak points as well for which we do not hate them, but which we recognize ...

Many brutalities were committed by the eventual victors. Still ... Auschwitz and Buchenwald? There is no balancing of accounts. Naturally not. The scales are too different. These facts are but the two sides of the one truth that "Hitler is within us." This is our fiercest accusation against National Socialism: that it set up the ultimate evil within all of us as the principle of order, as a system: the ultimate evil within all of us. We come out of a world in which Nuremberg is not enough, in which deeds must match the tribunal in order to eliminate Hitler; and to eliminate war with him.

War is a deception because it seeks to persuade people that they themselves, not the systems, want conflicting objectives. This is a lie. After all, all people want the same. They want to live, to satisfy their hunger and quench their thirst; and they long for love and happiness. We have so much in common. The war fronts run the wrong way. Until now, they have run between nations. However, the fronts should be directed against our common faults, against the artificial intolerance which breaks up the genuine communities that are rooted in objectivity and not in nationalism; against systems which would cheat us out of the things we have in common and would make our ideals the slaves of our faults.This is our second dreadful accusation against National Socialism: it has defrauded us of our ideals. We believed in our country, in honor, loyalty, courage and obedience. The National Socialists perverted everything. Everything. It is no small matter to be cheated out of the ideals in which one believed.

A soldier lost and alone in "boundlessness" longs for other men, because the spaciousness overpowers him, the individual. He even longs for the enemy. We made the great discovery that one is as lonely when one is a particle of dust as when one is an individual in the "boundlessness." For to be free also means not to be alone.

Thus we returned brimful with mental pictures from the lumber camps of Canada, the cotton fields of Alabama, the coal mines of France and the armament factories beyond the Ural Mountains. We came out of the "boundlessness" and found ourselves in the narrowness of bounds at home, the narrowness of both men and imaginations.

When we returned home we thought we could just step in and work. This turned out to be an illusion, because the homeland turned out to be quite different from what we had expected. The people at home wanted us to return and they thought that we were needed. This, too, was an illusion, because we were quite different from what they had expected. Our pictures were different from theirs. We tried to digest them inwardly and to grope our way into the future. They, especially the politicians, tried to start from the point where the development had once been interrupted. They are afraid of our war experiences and forget that many of us only had experiences during the war.

Whenever we turn to their politics they grow suspicious; and when we deviate from "the line," their line, they all too readily call us "inexperienced," "dangerous" and, perhaps depending on their point of view, even Fascists and militarists; and try to do away with us as soon as possible. In their next speech, though, they proclaim: "We have got to win the youth!" We are neither Fascists nor militarists, neither reactionary nor obstinate. We are just different.

Some time ago we were told by a young American who had fought in the Pacific and was now in the occupation forces in Germany: "I am spoiled for my country. It's too narrow." His country: the immense plains, forests and mountain ranges in the United States! While he spoke there was a strange expression in his eyes. We understood each other right away.

Rüdiger Proske's war horizon was wider than mine, to be sure. His encompassed the endless land to the east and the horrible suffering of both Russian and German soldiers. Luckily, I was spared the Russian experience.

Father had been on the eastern front for better than two years. While a fellow prisoner in Crossville, Tennessee, he had described for me, vividly and persuasively, the similarities between Russia and the USA: the vast plains, the endless fields, the sparse population, the extreme seasons and the stark colors. Father was knowledgeable in geography and history -- and an astute observer.

In many ways, in the first four or five years of the post-war era, I identified with Proske's perceptions and definitions, and with his hopes and frustrations about the role of returned soldiers in the fledgling new democracy. There was his juxtaposition of boundlessness and bounds, mirroring both my *Fernweh* and my discipline. There was his notion, no, imperative, to consider friend and foe equally human and worthy of respect; and that the frontlines between warring nations be transformed into common fronts against intolerance, nationalism and corrupting systems. Proske spoke to my mind and heart in these years of finding and ordering my new life with its different values, tasks and associations.

And so, in 1949, I wrote to a newspaper editor in Coblence who, I felt, was unjustly chastising the former soldiers and, equally biased, heaping praise on the emerging leaders many of whom had spent the Hitler years in hibernation, however lonesome and difficult they may have been for their aging bodies and still hopeful hearts. My letter was entitled: "Politics, Policies, Democracy -- and How the Younger Generation Sees

Them." I went on to take him to task for only lamenting and not staking out principles, policies and politics for the future.

"The parties of today," I said, "are those of the day before yesterday. We do not and cannot trust them. They cater to special interests. There are several parties, instead of only two as in the time-tested democracies of Great Britain and the USA.

"Very few of us have time for politics. We are picking up yesterday's pieces. Out of the rubble we want to build a new house, a new life. We have little time for things marginal. After years of struggle and danger we would like, even for short hours, to dance, to have fun and simply to relax."

In hopes that my editor friend might publish excerpts from my letter -- a vain hope, it turned out to be -- I called upon my young fellow citizens who were still standing aside in bitterness and internal turmoil to help build a new democratic Germany. I called upon our elders: "The God of History has judged National Socialism and the German nation in which it was born. In the eyes of the world we Germans are deemed to be bad people. Don't make us any worse because you can neither forget nor forgive. Rightly or wrongly, you still carry the responsibility: show us the way, a more constructive, more reasonable, more democratic way!"

To assure continuity to this recording of my political interest, I have hurried ahead to 1949. It is necessary to return to the spring of 1947, for crucial changes in my life were imminent. Not that I foresaw them clearly. Nor that I had planned them.

STUDYING AND ASSESSING

Always looking forward to the weekends with soccer, dancing and "girls" in Weilburg made the lonely and hungry weekdays in Marburg more bearable, but only barely so. My study book for the summer of 1946 listed philology -- the study of languages -- as my major. There was an advanced course in English: essay-writing and translation; two classes in French syntax and "oral-language exercises"; and, a tribute to my special interest in the Middle East and experience in North Africa -- the latter surely distorted by war -- Arabic for beginners. There were also two Spanish courses for beginners and "less practiced."

When reporting on my high-school years in *Under the Crooked Cross* I devoted attention to my then teachers, their idiosyncrasies and the extent of their identification with the ways of National Socialism. I will do the same here. In 1946 and 1947 it was critical for teachers, government officials, clergymen and lawyers alike to appear not only "democratic" under the watchful eyes of the occupation authorities but openly anti-Nazi, whatever their often checkered past or, in a few cases, their luckily untainted professional lives.

Professor de Ituribaría was a slight Mediterranean-looking and balding man of undefined age. He claimed to be Basque. I entertained the thought that he might have come to Germany in the late thirties as an admirer of its new ways. But being Basque, he may have tried to get away from the bloody struggle between Franco's *Falange* and the Spanish Republicans.

Dr. Schimmel was in her mid-thirties, a plump and friendly woman. She wore glasses and had the studious and slightly abstract ways of an intellectual. To this novice in a non-European language, and most systematic Arabic at that, a sharp, logical and retentive mind was required to get into it. I never really did: Arabic was too alien, too difficult to pronounce and perhaps too outlandish a subject to contribute to a career once my studies were done.

The four or five of us in Dr. Schimmel's class struggled with such oddities of a language that has no clear vowels, runs right to left, construes verbs indirectly by relating nouns to adjectives and conjunctions, and has rigid declinations -- I believe twelve -- for nouns derived from basic three-consonant words. Dr. Schimmel, so knowledgeable, so much inside "her" Arabic, struggled no less with our uncomprehending and slow minds.

Still, I got at least a whiff of the beauty of Arabic: not in the ways it sounds, so guttural, but in the infinite variety, yet almost mathematical logic, of its syntax. It was little wonder, therefore, that I was attracted to and, indeed, copied dozens of medieval writings and ornaments called arabesques. From simple handsome script in the ninth and tenth centuries the letters began to flower in ever new yet repetitive designs of blossoms, buds, vines and leaves growing tendrils around the stark letters.

Ever so vaguely, I began to sense the intimate and profound relationship between "the Arab mind" and Arabic: its logic, its magic like that of a mirage, and its breathtaking achievements in architecture, art, mathematics, medicine and, strangely, its greater religious tolerance than medieval -- and later -- Christians could muster.

Although still veiled from my Western and European comprehension but informed by my own encounter with the desert, its clarity and solitude, I began to understand why, to them, the Arabs and their language, living in the narrow strip between the desert and the sea -- the Fertile Crescent -- were bound to develop such a logical and systematical language.

Westerners born to different geography, climates, history and "softer" languages see in the stubborn logic of Arabs, who might argue about and fight over the rectitude of "one of the Prophet's hairs" for centuries, nothing but a narrow stupidity and dangerous fanaticism. But for me, out of the love for the desert and my beginning grasp of "the Arab mind" there grew a lifelong attraction to the world of Islam ... the essence of Arabic and Arabian culture.

Dr. Schimmel died in 2005. A rare half-page obituary in *The New York Times* was devoted to her. She had become a world-renowned expert on the Arab world and its ways. An adviser to the House of Saud and other Middle Eastern potentates, it turned out that she was three years younger than I!

Arabesques

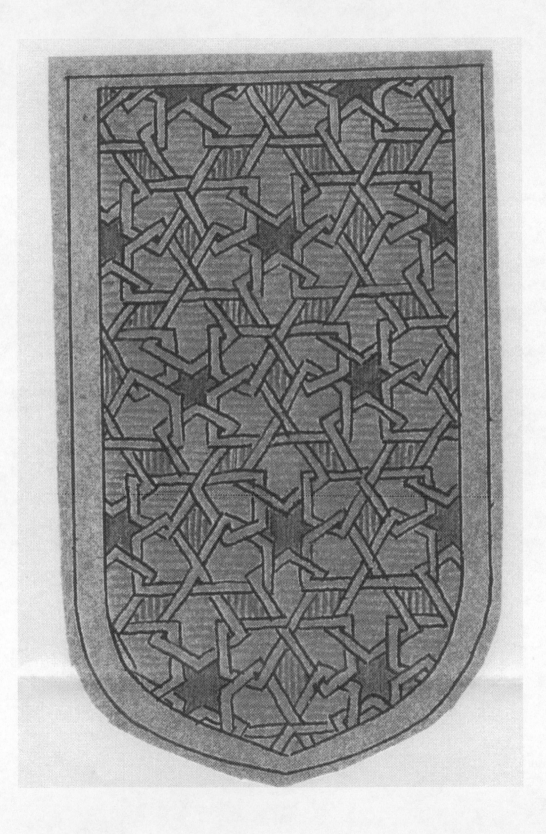

61

However, this chronicler must not stray from his story and, like Lawrence of Arabia, ride off on one of his favorite and possibly fancied hobby-horses.

Easily the most interesting and likable teacher was a Dr. Schneider. He was around 37, a handsome man with an open face, blond and rather long hair and inspiring teaching skills. His English was of the British rather than the American intonation and near-flawless. He might have been an interpreter in German intelligence or a POW camp in Great Britain. I did wonder why at his age and with his Nordic looks he did not seem to be tainted by National Socialism, as so many and those unemployed teachers were. Never mind, he was both good and popular.

Essay-writing took turns with reading English and American newspapers, and written translations into English. No German word was spoken in his class, which was well-attended. I remember one translation of an obituary for some well-known pre-Hitler German politician. Only one of some twenty students, but not I, hit upon the proper title, "in memoriam." But then, this is not exactly a household word.

One of the students in Dr. Schneider's class was a rather plain full-figured young woman by the name of Brigitta Wagner. We took a liking to each other, centered mostly on our English homework. It was a platonic thing, although she once came to Löhnberg, a fat farming village near Weilburg with a much better soccer teaam than ours, to watch me play; better mostly, because farmers had meat, butter and milk and could thus attract much better players! We lost 3:1. *Fräulein* Wagner did not take to soccer; and my "social life," on weekends, was in Weilburg anyhow.

HEIDI

The miserable winter of 1946-47 was going by all too slowly in my life's three compartments: study in Marburg, soccer-and-dance weekends in Weilburg and Christmas holidays in Coblence. The Weilburg soccer club had ascended to the regional league and played well in the middle pack of the teams. I continued to spend Friday and Saturday nights in Schnupp's sleazy café and mostly unmade attic beds. Butchers Heinen, Knuppertz -- their wives were sisters -- and Wirtz provided ample and fat meals, of which I could only dream, and did, in Marburg and Cappel. A starveling student, they knew, was less than top-fit for tough soccer matches. So, in a way, I became their soccer retainer.

It was hard to concentrate on my studies: the long hike to and from the university, the less than friendly landlord, the often cold room, the subsistence rations and the lack of conviction as to where my studies were leading -- to being a teacher, of all things? -- all bore down on my normally happy disposition.

I remember well the occasions when, making a little detour in the morning, I would walk by the American PX building in Marburg. Through the grids of the basement windows the most delicious scent of fresh-baked doughnuts would well up. I would stop briefly and fill my lungs with it.

The noon meal at one or two inexpensive eateries frequented by students consisted of potatoes in different forms and some cabbage, turnips or spinach. About twice a week I could afford a little gravy or melted margarine: that took a five-gram "fat" coupon. In the evening, then, some bread, milk and cold cuts bought with more coupons. Little wonder, therefore, that I looked forward to the ample weekend feasts!

It must have been in December 1946, when, one cold Monday morning, I took the train back to Marburg for another week of less than inspiring study and a less than full stomach. Let me tell the story the way I later wrote it up in my little notebook. It was to be a chance encounter with Heidi who would, ten months later, be my wife.

Heidi: what does she look like? When I have told all, you are likely to know what she looks like, what she meant to me, and means now. So, listen!

I had known her for quite some time, had seen her often when, with a dark-haired fellow she was a spectator at our soccer matches. I knew that she could look straight into my eyes and that her laughter was free and clear; and that when she laughed, small dimples would form around her mouth.

She was an East Prussian, I had heard. And I had danced with her, once or twice. She danced lightly. In dancing with her the nearness of her body was neither intriguing nor intoxicating, but it was nice to dance with her; as yet, somehow, impersonal.

When I took that Monday morning train she, the East Prussian, as I simply called her, took the same train. I talked to her and we sat down in the same compartment.

I remember clearly: it was a re-built freight car with new windows. It was comfortably warm. We laughed and talked silly stuff, as young people might. Certainly, I tried to make a good impression. Did we understand each other intuitively? I do not think so.

Before she left the train at the next station stop I asked her as I would have, and had, asked many a nice girl: "Would you care to go dancing with me?" "Yes." "Good, I'll come by after the Christmas vacation." Her hand was small and well kept. Its grip was both firm and gentle. Ever since, I like her hands.

The train started to move. There she walked, parallel to the tracks. Now, she disappeared behind a pile of logs. There she was again. I waved. She waved back -- in the way women might wave whom one does not easily forget: with a light motion and with a smile around her mouth and in her eyes; not at all full of promise but full of grace. More from lack of a dance partner than wanting to see her, the East Prussian, I went by her house after Christmas. In fact, I did not know her name nor her address, but I found out; it was Heidi and she lived in that house on the main road.

Heidi? Yes, Heidi. Her family name was written on a small card on the entrance door: Brien. Heidi Brien: sounds good. I rang the bell; and was not as sure of myself as I pretended to be. Heidi opened herself. That first evening we went dancing. It was a lovely evening, what with her playful eyes and her dimples, our young abandon and her light-of-foot dancing, which did not intoxicate but felt good.

It was not far to her house but we took a little detour. "Please, just a little detour." For it was bitter cold. Was it on this first evening or on one of those following which we danced, laughed and talked away that I asked her on the way home: "May I give you a kiss?" -- using the formal *Sie*. I do not remember any more.

Her answer, half mischievous and half teasing, was like many of her responses. One did not know whether they were spoken seriously or jokingly. But this time, her reply lifted her suddenly above all the other women with whom I had spent my evenings. It was a rogue's answer all right but it was straightforward, clear and courageous: "Yes, that would be very nice!" "Excuse me, (again with the formal *Sie*) but after that response I must collect myself first."

And then we kissed; and kissed often that evening. And her kiss was like her dancing and like her hands. In her kiss was everything: the smile in her eyes, the dimples and the knowledge: I am young and I am pretty. The kiss did not intoxicate. It did not make the world around disappear. It was light and tender and hard to forget.

We went out together often. Because I knew that she understood me I talked much about myself, the years as a soldier, my plans, my dreams. She was a good listener. She would look at me with dark and clear eyes which said: "Yes, I understand you." And yet, she could laugh disbelievingly, or rascally and sillily, and say: "How could you say a thing like that?"

Or: "I would like to dance."

Heidi had begun to occupy my senses, which like to gauge and order things. Not that I thought only of her. But now and then I did; and I thought: either she really likes me or she only wants to play with me -- with me who wanted to appear so seasoned and was yet so young. Or perhaps, she only wanted a man.

One evening -- we sat in my dimly lit café and I had allowed her to look into my very soul -- I told her what I had been thinking. I thought of myself as some kind of hero, being so frank. But when I mentioned the last choice of her just wanting a man, I became suddenly conscious of what I had said and thought. And I sensed that she struggled with the answer; and felt how much I had offended her. When she remained silent, when I thought that tears would come to her eyes, when I knew for sure that I had behaved like a swine so to think and speak, I could only beg: "Can you forgive me? If not, if not, it would be better I left."

Heidi remained silent, for quite a while still, which seemed unusually long to me. There was no impatience in me as I waited for her reply, because I felt that she would forgive me. And she did: with a long kiss in which there were both her smile and her tears.

It was this evening, I believe, that I asked her to pick me up at the train from Marburg. Ever since, when I sit in the evening train to Weilburg, I can no longer sleep, for I know that someone dear is waiting for me. In my mind's eye I see her standing in the corridor in front of the ticket booth, see her in her gray overcoat, feel her hand, firm and tender at once.

I know how difficult it is for her to pick me up, go for a walk or dance. Heidi is not well. Her heart acts up, and she has swollen and aching joints. She winces when someone kicks her inadvertently while dancing. I see how in her pretty face pain and smile are contending with each other for a moment.

Last Sunday Mother visited Weilburg. It so happened that Mother and Heidi were to take the same train. I picked Heidi up in the morning to take her to the station. We walked arm in arm, like a young married couple. I told her that Mother was on her train, too, and that I would introduce her. Heidi made droll objections: no, she would rather travel by herself. She looked very young. "Mother" -- she was already at the station, and I recognized her right away by the red kerchief -- "This is Heidi Brien."

What Mother and Heidi said I do not remember any more. But I had a strange feeling: three people are together, three people forming a triangle with me in the middle, while the first and the third are still weighing and probing each other. This feeling became stronger when I copied a few train departures for Mother, and Heidi, who had already bought her ticket, joined us. The question was: is one person in this triangle not one too many? Is one person not a stranger? And here I had thought that I could be a smiling spectator when two people dear to me would meet. That spectator role had to be abandoned, I knew suddenly, because I was a spectator no longer. I had become one of the principals. This realization made me uncomfortable.

In the evening, then, I picked both of them up: a mother whose face looked old and tired, but happy, under that red kerchief; and a girl whose eyes were beaming under that wide-rimmed hat. Illuminated by a street light, Heidi's mouth was small and red, with dimples around it.

The last stretch of the way home Mother and I walked alone. She said good-bye with a slightly pained smile: it was probably right that a mother leaves and the young people stay together. Did she really know how true that is?

Heidi is still sick, quite sick. Yet at Easter time she hardly missed a dance because she might have felt that my eyes would wander; and because -- well, maybe she really loves me. Maybe? No, I know she does.

And I? She means much to me, very much. Sometimes I long for her, for her fine hands, her smile. Sometimes I think: yes, this is the woman I would want forever. But then I question myself: Marry? And I feel: that might be happiness. But I also feel: that might be the end of all plans, all dreams. The distant white cities and blue seas with the sun's bright light and dark shades will die. Nothing will be left but a longing which, I know, will never be fulfilled.

Since yesterday when we walked home together and kissed I know how much I love her, this Heidi. And I said after a long kiss, which was as light and gentle as her hands and yet intoxicating like strong, sweet wine: "I would like to have all of you, all." She understood.

The cobblestone street in front of Heidi's door was uneven and her feet were hurting from much dancing. This gave her the feeling that, after another kiss, she might fall. I asked: "Are you afraid to fall?" "Yes." "But why?" "Because I would have to get up alone!" Was this not the answer to my question: "I would like to have all of you, all?"

Later I asked her as I had done often: "Heidi, isn't there something you want to tell me still?" Because I knew that this was so. "Yes, there is." But then, someone came down the narrow street with long strides. They intruded. "Don't you want to tell me?" "When he is gone." The someone walked by, turned the corner. It was quiet again, very quiet. But she was still silent. Then, finally, swallowing: "No, I have nothing to say."

So little do I know about the woman named Heidi, whom I love.

(Later that spring in Coblence) It has gotten late. Father sits on the other side of the table, reading. The kitchen clock ticks. A motorbike purrs by. I think of Heidi and want to give her this little story. And I long for her smile, her hands and her kisses.

By the middle of the 1947 spring semester my interest in the language studies was waning rapidly, in spite of my normal discipline to apply myself. Because of my soccer connections, my life was probably less hungry than that of many students. I was healthy and strong, unlike so many who had been shot up during the war. Marburg had several hospitals and rehabilitation centers. Two incidents are remembered.

The tramcar was moving into the city: standing room only. All riders were visibly preoccupied with the cares of the day. Into the heavy silence, the voice of an ex-soldier: "Just keep kicking my leg, lady; it is a wooden one!"

Three invalids were coming toward me in the street arm-in-arm, talking and laughing: one with the yellow armband of the blind and a scar on his temple; the second limping on a prosthesis; and the third with a claw at the end of his artificial arm. All three seemed to have a good time. Or did they?

The soccer season was ending. May 1 was approaching, an official holiday in Germany. I had invited Heidi to Marburg: to see my bachelor quarters in Cappel, to visit the medieval city and to enjoy the holiday together. The weather favored us. It was a lovely day in the Lahn valley.

We walked the good mile from the Marburg South station to Cappel. I introduced Heidi to the Groeb family: *Frau* Groeb sporting a fresh apron, *Herr* Groeb his usual grouchy self. I borrowed a second chair, so that we could sit and talk a while in my small upstairs room -- when an unexpected and protracted problem arose.

The Groebs' seven-year-old daughter, sneaky and mischievous at best, insisted on accompanying us: what was the student and his girl up to in his room? After a while when I thought that her understandable curiosity had been satisfied, I asked her politely to leave. Not only did she refuse. She crawled under the bed. She had to be dragged out, kicking and screaming. Later on, Heidi and I had an enjoyable walk through the hillside city, up to the castle. We spent ten grams of "fat" coupons on a richer-than-normal supper.

It must have been in the last weeks of what was to be my final semester in Marburg that I had a morning date with Mother. Coming from Weilburg, she was to meet me around 8 A.M. in Giessen, 25 miles down-river from Marburg. Was it a Sunday? The first train out of Marburg South did not go. I had no way of reaching Mother, and the next train did not leave much before noon.

Brooding over my dilemma, I saw a G.I. mail train pull into the station, MPs jumping down and positioning themselves along the special mail coaches, submachine guns cradled in their arms. It was obvious that they were taking their duty seriously. Take that train? A quick decision: yes! The stationmaster blew his whistle and raised his green disc. The guards climbed up. I jumped onto the platform of the last car, the accordion-like contraption that connected coaches partly hiding my presence.

How to get off the train in Giessen? Terrible fear for half an hour. My luck held: outside the station, the train stopped at a signal. I jumped off and ran across the tracks -- to greet Mother with a broad smile and that "wild story." As I look back over my life, this was probably the most courageous -- and foolhardy -- thing I ever did!

The spring semester ended in the first days of July. I had taken a total of sixteen hours -- there were no credits in the German system --: eight a week in four English courses; four hours in French, one of them called "exercises relating to Marie of France," whoever she was; and four with an Arabic flavor provided by that mild-mannered and bespectacled Dr. Schimmel, who was at her best in a colloquium on "Issues in the History of Islam." By then my mind was pretty much made up not to return to the learned and, in some cases, stuffy halls of the Phillips *Universität*!

It was probably in late June that, after an evening's dancing and much kissing, I "smuggled" Heidi into my attic room at Schnupp's. We made real love -- and on a bed -- for the first time. It was exciting, exhilarating and ever so natural. Our time had come, our time together, probably for good.

In July I was in Coblence, with Heidi. Were the parents away, for a week's vacation? At any rate, the two of us, by now sleeping together on whatever rare occasions offered themselves, enjoyed our stay and ate as much fruit as the large garden would provide. Indeed, ripening apples were spread on the floor of what might be called the minister's official parlor. Furniture was sparse. I do remember the room for the lovemaking and the pervasive scent of delicious apples.

Well, Richard and Gerda also came for a couple of days. The four of us had long, animated and often funny talks about the merits -- and demerits -- of living together and of marrying, after all. And so, half eager and half hesitant, Heidi and I shared equally in the decision to get engaged. The parents returned. They seemed to appreciate it. I say "seemed" because it would turn out that Mother, perhaps prejudiced in her middle-class status of a minister's wife, was to provide many instances of unfriendliness toward Heidi, albeit rarely to her face.

Still, from the valuable treasure of Mother's family inheritance which had, none too soon, escaped the bombing raids on Coblence and the complete destruction of our home, two pure-gold rings were given to Heidi and me as engagement present. The date of August 12, 1947, was properly engraved in them. Would it not be nice, and right, if Granddaughter Julia and her future fiancé might thus wear the wedding bands of Grandfather Grunwald and Oma from the year 1882? (Yes, Julia and Tom now wear them.)

Opa and Oma Brien

BOOK TWO:
THE GERMAN MIRACLE

A JOB

With marriage ahead and little ambition left for the continuation of my studies, I found it necessary to look around for work -- even though money earned was of little use in the economy, all of it miserable. A quick solution offered itself.

For some time one of Father's tasks had been to be the Coblence representative of Evangelisches Hilfswerk, a relief effort made through Protestant parishes along the Rhine and Moselle to help the neediest among the thousands who were hungry or lacked the bare necessities: with used clothing, blankets, food and CARE packages sent from America. As usual, Father threw himself into this task with much energy and organizational talent.

His "partner" was a mild-mannered bespectacled American clergyman by the name of Ray Maxwell: in his late thirties, unmarried, in well-pressed suits and well-polished shoes perhaps five foot nine, an avid smoker and quite limited German. It so happened that the Rev. Raymond E. (Ebersole) Maxwell, an Episcopal priest from Hannibal, Missouri, and regional representative of Church World Service, was about to lose his trusted secretary who, having been "cleansed" from former Party membership, was anxious to return to teaching.

Well, Mr. Maxwell interviewed me. He found my English acceptable, my lack of secretarial skills less of a handicap than I had feared and my station as a son of a Protestant pastor promising for the job. My views on religion, in general, and church work, in particular, were not probed. If Mr. Maxwell had any knowledge of or doubt about Father's tainted background as a Party member and an officer in a National Socialist service organization, he did not say. October 1, 1947, was set as the date for starting out as his "private secretary."

The wages would be 250 worthless *Reichsmark* and an extraordinarily precious CARE package each month. It contained such unattainable and half-forgotten valuables as butter, coffee, cocao, chocolate or, as variants, two blankets or cloth for a suit and linen for bedding.

Fed up with the seeming dead end of language study, compelled by the new prospect of being a provider and enticed by such "wages" in a climate of not-enough-to-eat and useless money, I quickly accepted what looked like an interesting, personable and rewarding engagement.

The wedding date was set for November 27, 1947. Father would officiate at the "church" wedding. We applied for a license at the Coblence city marriage office. The official in charge was an elderly, portly and officious man, probably reinstated after having "missed" the Hitler years. His name was Zwick, and his name seemed to suit him. In German "Zwick" means complicated and tricky. He was both -- and the bureaucrat incarnate.

As a refugee whose family had fled before the Russian advance in the winter of 1945 with no more possessions than what her mother and sister could carry on their backs, Heidi had no papers to prove her identity save her military pay-book. She had a statement notarized that she was born on October 12, 1923, in Rositten, County of Preussisch-Eylau, East Prussia. It caused *Herr* Zwick to raise his brows and heave a tiny sigh. "This is not acceptable in lieu of a birth certificate. You see, realistically, you were not present at your birth; your mother would have to provide such a statement." Eventually, his scruples were overcome.

Busy fall months. On weekends I played soccer in Weilburg. During the week I stayed with the parents and rode my bike to and from work. Through the connections of influential soccer friends we were promised one large room in a stately house on Limburgerstrasse. Even the tiniest living space was controlled by the authorities. Another soccer "patron," *Herr* Müller, owner of a practically empty clothing store, would yet provide a "wool-based" navy-blue suit, secure a combination of coal-burning oven-stove and two narrow beds with mattresses. Early in November Heidi and I pushed the stove up the steep and long grade of Limburgerstrasse, a considerable piece of labor. There were few occasions to wear the "good" suit. It was also very scratchy!

The wedding day came cool, wet and misty, snow mixing with the drizzle. No wedding gown, no tuxedo, no church service with ushers and bridesmaids. The "parlor" was the place. Father said a few and heartfelt words. And off we were, Heidi and I, to the city license bureau, better than two miles away.

The shortcut path along the slope of the Moselle was slippery. Heidi almost fell into one of the many bomb craters. If Father was brief, *Herr* Zwick was long, pompous and pseudo-religious, exalting the blessed state of matrimony. A shriveled lady played the piano. We exchanged vows and rings. The rules of church and state had been satisfied: we were married and on our common way.

Winter was approaching. A supply of wood and coal came "sub-rosa" via the soccer club, as came a table, a couple of chairs and an old wardrobe. And so Heidi and I set out on our journey, weekends only, in a once-handsome room looking down upon Limburgerstrasse and across the river to the baroque castle and hilltop town.

We were young, strong, resourceful -- and very happy. Who cared how rudimentary were our quarters and how tenuous our circumstances.

But what about my new work?

Mainzerstrasse 19 had once been a stately four-story turn-of-the-century house, one of the very few on Mainzerstrasse not completely flattened by the heavy bombing raids in 1944. On my first day of work for Ray Maxwell and Church World Service, October 1, 1947, while still looking better than most houses on the mile-long Mainzerstrasse, Number 19 was reduced to two stories and a haphazard roof; "haphazard" because it kept raining in. Several containers were strategically placed to catch water dripping from the ceiling. The Werneckes, elderly and once wealthy owners of a furniture store, lived on the ground floor. Furniture was Spartan. The manual typewriter was all right. To this day, though, my typing is of the two-finger variety. In many years of ample practice I have picked up good speed.

There was a telephone, two desks, some chairs, a table and a worn sofa. Some food and clothing supplies were stored in a corner.

Ray Maxwell, meticulously attired and cheerfully puffing away, initiated me to Church World Service. It was a cooperative U.S. agency founded in 1946 to pool the resources of most Protestant churches. Catholic Relief Services, Lutheran World Relief, the Mennonite Central Committee and the American Friends Service Committee (Quakers) had successfully lobbied the U.S. Government for permission to help the suffering populace. They had overcome views quite strongly held by some American leaders that

Germany should never recover. These agencies had formed a consortium: CRALOG, the Council of Relief Agencies Licensed to Operate in Germany. Ray Maxwell and two other Americans had been sent to the French Zone early in 1947.

It had seemed necessary and right to distribute relief through established German counterpart agencies that were little, if at all, tainted by National Socialism: Caritas, Evangelisches Hilfswerk and Arbeiterwohlfahrt (Workers' Welfare League). So Ray spent much time with his German partners: a middle-aged alert Catholic Monsignor, my father and a plump motherly lady from Arbeiterwohlfahrt. He also spent much time with other Protestant clergy, learning German and delving into the altogether different history and patterns of the German territorial churches.

In this emerging network of cooperation and affinity, Dr. Sachsse, Father's superior, played an important part. He was a man of Father's age, usually dressed in a frock-coat: tall, friendly, sharp and smooth at once, like any good politician, and untained by National Socialism. Obviously he had all the prerequisites for relating to the heavy-footed and unfriendly French military government and the leaders of the Church of the Rhineland, with headquarters in distant Düsseldorf in the British Zone. Many and large institutions, from hospitals to asylums, were church-owned and -operated; and most of their inmates were in dire straights.

With the rank of lieutenant colonel, unsoldierly Ray Maxwell kept close to the Religious Affairs' office of the U.S. military government in Frankfurt. Not only did he have PX privileges. He drove -- at least from our perspective -- a huge American car and spent much time with two mechanics on Viktoriastrasse to keep his cruiser afloat. I learned quickly that reading the daily paper, in his case the Paris-based Herald Tribune, was a sacred duty and instant right! Without his paper, Mr. Maxwell seemed to be less cheerful and focused. Indeed, he would drive the forty miles to the nearest PX in Limburg for his daily injection of news!

He must also have spent some time with a certain 30-year old German lady, sister to one of my classmates killed in the war, a statuesque divorced woman who happened to be the local "coal czarina" of the City of Coblence. Ray Maxwell had his quarters with the Wilmses on Ludwigstrasse. Ilse was their daughter. But for more than a year I had no inkling that something was blossoming between staunch bachelor Ray and alluring divorcée Ilse, who had a "superbrat" of a son by the most Aryan of names, Sigurd.

Under Maxwell's friendly tutelage I quickly learned the ropes: the office routine of manning the 'phone, typing, filing and interpreting; also, the context of partners in Bremen, where shipments of relief goods arrived, in New York and in Geneva.

Ray was a wonderful, patient, sometimes funny and always pastoral man of considerable learning -- and atrocious yet undaunted German. His slender and almost effeminate fingers made an art of lighting and holding a cigarette, to be quickly matched by the deep satisfaction of inhaling its smoke. Soon, he acquired a cigarette-holder which he handled not unlike the late Franklin Delano Roosevelt!

Ray hailed from a part Pennsylvania Dutch family in Greensburg, PA. His father and uncles ran the large furniture store in town. Ray had spent a few years at a Quaker school in Ramallah, Palestine; and he was most knowledgeable about the Middle East and Eastern Orthodox churches, in particular. This background helped him in the mid-fifties to become the secretary for the Middle East with the World Council of Churches, by then well established in Geneva, Switzerland.

It probably was in early December 1947, when his -- and my -- reputation were publicly tested. On a bitter-cold day the "Friendship Train" was due to stop in Coblence-Lützel. A few cars were to be uncoupled for the distribution of relief goods in the Coblence-Treves area. Grain, canned meat, vegetables and margarine had been gathered in the U.S. Midwest, many carloads full, and shipped to Bremerhaven: a visible and most welcome display of American generosity.

A shivering crowd. Willi Stöck, an emerging radio reporter and one-time fellow *Pimpf*, was there. So were all sorts of church and civic leaders, and a few French officers. Ray said a few words in English, mangled by my embarrassingly poor French. And then, in a warm and comfortable train coach along the Rhine to Mainz for another distribution stop of the "Friendship Train." Looking out of the window, I was strangely torn between the sheer luxury of the "occupiers" in the coach and my assertive identification with the "occupied," the people in the familiar towns and villages, barely looking up from their chores: cold, sullen and, most of them, hungry. Indeed, for an hour I traveled in two altogether different worlds, enjoying one but belonging to the other.

The "no-potato" winter of 1947-48, cold and wet at that, was a time as miserable as might befall a Western nation. Money was worthless. No goods could be had, except on the black market. Mainzerstrasse was desolate -- with few cars, all of them belonging to the French military and civilian administrators. Their commandant, an ordinary-looking man with glasses, must yet have had one house rebuilt. In it, across the street, lived his mistress, so went the story, a very attractive Jewish woman who had miraculously escaped death in a concentration camp.

Surely and in spite of the grim winter for me -- and now for Heidi and me -- life had changed drastically. "Home" with the parents during the work-week, I was yet coming "home" each Friday to our Spartan place in Weilburg: to play soccer, eat well and, much more important, be in love with my beautiful and cheerful wife. Misery all around us, we were yet happy in our small world of talking, dancing, listening, laughing and loving. Better things to come were but a matter of time.

And so, once again, inevitably and with new hope, a dismal winter would turn into spring, the spring of 1948.

Sunday, June 20, was a warm spring day. All was new and green and blossoming. A friendship match in Usingen: an easy victory. And yet on that Sunday evening, as I took the train back to Coblence -- the Lahn bridge near Balduinstein was still out, a small boat making the connection -- there was already in my mind and heart the burden of separation from Heidi and of the chores in the still rubble-strewn city of Coblence.

In total secrecy, plans for a currency reform had been drawn up by Dr. Hjalmar Schacht, recently found innocent at Nuremberg and his experts, both foreign and domestic, to devaluate the worthless *Reichsmark* and introduce the new *Deutschmark*, at a ratio of ten to one. And each civilian would receive forty new Marks.

Dr. Schacht, then around 75, had been the architect of the revaluation of the Mark after the Great Inflation of 1923. With one stroke of genius, albeit backed by the latent skill and will of a downtrodden nation, the "German miracle" was about to begin on that June day in 1948.

On the first Monday of a new era, then, what miracle: new wares at new prices in many stores, juicy cherries at ridiculously low cost, luxury things like radios, watches and cigarettes for sale! My bank account, or one tenth of it, had suddenly acquired real worth and hence different meaning. Although the future, under foreign occupation, with dismantling continuing in the Russian Zone and little authority in German hands, was far from clear or assured, all Germans sensed that better times were at hand.

From Church World Service dollars traded at advantageous rates -- about one to four -- Ray "raised" my wages to one-hundred *Deutschmark*, in addition to the still crucial monthly CARE package.

Later that year the context of work began to change, if with the slow and cumbersome ways of international church organizations. It all began with the official founding of the World Council of Churches in the summer of 1948. Ray attended that auspicious event in Amsterdam as an observer and came back an even more convinced ecumenist.

Farsighted leaders in Geneva and New York began to realize that the relief phase in Europe might be over soon, rehabilitation and inter-church aid to take its place. WCC's first general secretary, Dr. Willem Visser t'Hooft, a towering theological mind and irrepressible social conscience behind a craggy face and with four or five languages at his disposal, added organizational talent and form to his many years of helping refugees from Hitler Germany, single-handedly.

At the same time, under the aegis of the recently formed United Nations' International Refugee Organization (IRO), millions of long-suffering Displaced Persons were either repatriated to Russia and other eastern European countries or, with rapid acceleration, resettled in the USA, Canada, Australia and Latin America.

The emerging Cold War made the former task difficult and onerous, and the latter necessary; and thousands of Displaced Persons languishing in camps off-limits to the German populace around them were caught in the vise between repatriation and resettlement.

Mostly financed by the IRO, CWS in Europe reached its zenith in a big Displaced Persons' operation with headquarters in Munich-Pasing. A fleet of vehicles, warehouses full of relief supplies, social services and substantial numbers of American expatriates cared for DPs in the American Zones of Germany, Austria and Italy.

In high quarters in Geneva and New York the decision had been taken to have WCC assume responsibility for refugee services in Europe and gradually phase out the heavy and "exterritorial" American presence. Down the line, Ray Maxwell was to combine refugee work for Germans with work for Displaced Persons, an almost unbridgeable assignment due to the historical and psychological chasm between one-time victors and victims.

Among the DP population, whole nationalities were caught at the end of the war between their former affinity with Hitler Germany and their eagerness now to distance themselves from it: Estonians, Latvians and Hungarians, in particular, but also some Russians and Rumanians who had thrown in their lot with the German armies retreating on the eastern front.

More, and more personal, changes lay ahead for Ray, Heidi and me. We all felt that this commuting business was not the best of arrangements. Some time in the fall of 1948 Ray succeeded with the French authorities, which could and did requisition housing, to have three rooms assigned to us in Arenberg, a village on high ground and with a Catholic pilgrimage shrine three miles northeast of Coblence.

Herr Frank, only recently come home after years as a POW in Russia, was a dour small man in his forties, his wife a non-descript housewife and his teen-age son in some apprenticeship. *Herr* Frank was an upholsterer. With a literally exploding market, he worked diligently in a shed behind his newish house. Why the long arm of the French authorities had chosen him to yield the upper floor to us was a mystery. He resented it bitterly; and our offer to have his son use the third room on "our" floor seemed to make little difference. After a year in Weilburg, then, we had a two-room apartment in Arenberg. There was no bathroom, I believe, and the toilet was halfway down the staircase.

During the winter of 1948-49 such never-dreamt-of items as motorcycles entered the marketplace. All our money and, for good measure, a CARE package went into "my" 125-ccm NSU, a gleaming, 4-1/2 horse two-stroke machine. From walking to cycling to riding a motorbike: things were looking up!

Somewhat earlier, though, there was even more important news: Heidi was expecting. By Christmas, heavy with child, she usually wore the only maternity dress she possessed. While I continued to play soccer in Weilburg, now for twenty *Deutschmarks* a clip and only a good hour's ride away, life as a family-to-be was becoming both normal and quite pleasant. In anticipation of that first child, why, it seemed appropriate to me to manufacture a plywood crib with, equally appropriate, inlaid arabesques and a simple "baldachin."

Early in January, though, Ray took me into his confidence with the startling and dismaying announcement: he would marry Ilse, the City "coal czarina." February 2 was set as the wedding date. A rather fancy restaurant in Rhens, overlooking the Rhine, was the place. "Dismayed" was a mild word for my apprehension, because Ray and I had developed an effective working relationship and mutual trust; and I was sure that the future Mrs. Maxwell disliked me as much as I did her. On my part, there was little rational cause for this -- except perhaps that I had intensely disliked her brother, a classmate who had been killed during the war. He had been a bully. The fact that Ray and I got along so well and that, unlike her brother, I had come out of the war alive may thus have been understandable reasons for her dislike.

That Mr. Maxwell needed special dispensation from his Episcopalian Church to marry a divorced woman bothered me less than him. I thought -- and still think so fifty years later -- that Ilse was a scheming and pushy woman whose sensuous looks and ways may well have overcome Ray's bachelor hesitations. That she strenuously objected to Heidi's only maternity dress worn on the festive occasion of her wedding did little to endear her to us. But then, it was a large and beautiful wedding: Ilse in a pale blue dress and Ray, somewhat uncomfortable, in a gray tuxedo.

Welcoming "Friendship Train," Koblenz-Lützel

Ilse and Ray Maxwell

February 1949

CORNELIA AND IRENE

In the early morning hours of April 29, 1949, our little Cornelia arrived in the Stiftskrankenhaus in Coblence. Not only had I made a plywood crib with jig-sawed arabesque inlays. That summer I made an album with just such a cover. The next few pages, then, will be excerpts from that record on how our first-born progressed. Pictures, little Cornelia, a crib, an album, a small apartment in Arenberg -- a young family on its way. The future held promise.

As Cornelia came to be the center of our family, things in Germany had already changed markedly. Let me sketch its rebirth -- before I return to our family chronicle.

The occupation powers still held sway in that spring of 1949, most severely in what was by then called the East Zone. The Russians' heavy hand and the beginning economic miracle in the three western zones caused many Easterners to flee to the west, a hazardous undertaking. Indeed, they and the more than two million earlier escapees from the former eastern provinces now located in Poland and Russia, who had settled in West Germany, became the powerful motor to rapid recovery.

Building and re-building everywhere. Mountains of rubble were carted away, streets cleared, railroad tracks laid, roads repaired, goods manufactured. In the Neuwied Basin, northwest of Coblence, conveyor belts and trucks hauled ten-foot layers of pumice-stone ashes away, day and night, to be turned into building blocks. Only a year after the currency reform, West Germany was humming with hope and bristling with energy.

To be sure, the Western Allies were helping -- and watching. The Russians' attempt to cut off supplies from the island of Berlin deep in the East Zone was thwarted by an air bridge of American, British and French cargo planes. In the summer of 1949 the Russians relented. At Tempelhof airfield in West Berlin a monument was raised to the success of the air bridge: a concrete contraption with three truncated rainbow-like arms. The Berliners, never lost for words, promptly called it the "Hunger Claw!"

1949 was to be the year, too, when out of the three western occupation zones and West Berlin, a *Bundesrepublik* (Federal Republic) would begin to take form from the ashes of the Third Reich and the shadows of the Weimar Republic. Such leaders as Konrad Adenauer and Theodor Heuss and, out of the resistance to Hitler, the Lord Mayor of West Berlin, Reuter, and later Chancellor Willi Brandt, were emerging. A few came, as I learned subsequently, from a school for a democratic Germany which the Americans had set up among anti-Hitler POWs in the USA, such as Professor Hallstein, one of the architects behind the "German miracle."

Aging Konrad Adenauer soon became a towering figure in West Germany. A devout Roman Catholic and Lord Mayor of Cologne in the twenties, he became a pillar of pro-Western sentiments and politics. Protestants from my native Oberberg region may be forgiven when they remembered, and loved to re-tell, the story of Adenauer's one-time "excursion" into our staunchly Protestant territory to be badly beaten up. Suspicion never left these Protestants that his affinity with the Western Allies was not entirely unrelated to the fact that had he maintained a more open stance toward people in the East Zone and German reunification, his narrow Catholic majority in West Germany would have been lost because of the Protestant majority in the east.

Some of us also thought that his lovely villa and rose garden in Königswinter had something to do with raising nearby and sleepy Bonn as the capital of the new Federal Republic.

With the Weimar leaders, its parties were returning: the Social Democrats, the Christian Democrats with their partners in Bavaria, the Christian Union, and the Free Democrats. In the rapidly heating-up Cold War and with the special blessing of the U.S. Government, the Communist Party was forbidden in West Germany. In East Germany one-time Communists had returned from their exile in Russia: Pieck, Ulbricht and Honecker, once tough anti-Nazi and now equally tough anti-West. And so, with all four Allies keeping a wary eye, the new "Democratic" Germanys and their antique leaders arose from the remnants and memories of the Weimar Republic, while most middle-aged men were still tainted by National Socialism and hence unable or unwilling to aspire to higher office.

How autocratic, even theocratic, "Old Man" Adenauer was may become graphic from three stories cherished by his fellow Rhinelanders, though Protestants more than Catholics.

Adenauer to his driver in the big Mercedes, on his way to some political event: "Karl, drive faster!" "But," says his chauffeur, "I am driving ninety-five miles already, Mr. Chancellor." "I did not tell you to drive ninety-five miles. I told you to 'drive faster!'"

The old CEO of a major Ruhr industry is retiring, slightly tainted by his early support of Adolf Hitler. The high-paying job is advertised. The chairman of the board makes it his business to interview the leading candidates himself. To the first: "I am quite impressed by your record and this interview. You'll certainly hear from us. But tell me: how much is three times four?" Like a pistol shot: "Twelve."

To the second, roughly the same compliments and the question: "How much is three times four?" A moment's hesitation, surprise: "Why -- twelve." "You'll hear from us, yes or no." Enters the third, a man of stellar anti-Nazi history. "And how much is three times four?" "Well, it depends: whether you calculate three times four or four times three. But I would have to say, twelve." Who do you think got the job? -- Konrad Adenauer's nephew!

Konrad Adenauer has a long one-on-one audience with the Pope. After a very long while, the cardinals outside the private chambers get worried about the two very old men inside. One of them dares peep through the keyhole. He sees Dr. Adenauer, tall, stern, standing erect -- and the Pope kneeling in front of him, his arms around the Chancellor's knees and his eyes looking up, begging: "But *Herr* Chancellor: I am Catholic already!" (Adenauer was so Catholic that he was trying to convert even the Pope to Catholicism.)

But back to little Cornelia, that wooden album and some excerpts from it. It is the spring of 1949.

Five weeks ago your mother and you came home from the hospital; that is, I brought you in the office car. And your mother had to get used to everything again. The first night your parents hardly closed their eyes. They listened to every breath, every sound coming from the crib.

Yes, the crib. I should have begun with that. The crib was your mother's idea. Whether the crib is still alive when you read these lines, Cornelia, I do not know. (It broke and was discarded in our move to Bad Homburg in 1951.) The crib was made of plywood, stained in different colors: bright Arabic letters with flowering vines on a dark background. At its head, another ornament: sixteen times Mohammed -- for your father was once a student of Arabic! A fine crib it was.

At birth you weighed about seven pounds. You had dark hair. It was only during your mother's hospital stay that we decided on your name. A child must have a name. How else could it be distinguished from other children? As you are very special, we came down with a very special name: Heide Cornelia. Heide resembles the name of your mother. We "stole" Cornelia. And who was she? She was the daughter of Scipio Africanus and the mother of the Gracchus brothers, living around 150 B.C. A real lady she was, so say the records.

Calling you Cornelia has already caused controversy. The city marriage-license office wanted to spell your name with a "K," just an ordinary "K." We protested. Now there is a petition in court to make sure that your name will be spelled with a "C." Imagine: you are only seven weeks old and already you have business in court. Eventually, the court ruled that the license office was "held to abide by the wishes of the parents, spelling Cornelia with a 'C' not being *abwegig*" (off the beaten path).

Five weeks have gone by. Already, you are a real charmer. But you have acquired a very bad habit. It has to do with your thumb. It is only a very small and rosy thumb, sucked red. There is also praise, though: although awake, you are quiet in the morning. So Mother can sleep a little longer. When your mother -- or anyone else -- approaches your crib your face beams, your legs kick and your arms flail. Your "drinking habits" have improved: a mere ten minutes to empty your bottle (with mother's milk). But then, you are right back to your thumb, a kind of *Ersatz* for your bottle.

Already, we are planning to "park" you when we go on vacation. You are simply too small to ride on a motorbike like your "big" cousin Regina. As of now, there are two applicants to take care of you: Aunt Gerda and "penny-pinching Oma." Everybody wants you -- except your parents.

Of late, we have occasionally left you alone, all by yourself. Most of the time you slept. Surely, you will understand that your parents would like to go to the movies, the tennis court or pick up fruits and vegetables in Engers.

Vegetables ... You are eating them already, even if you roll your eyes, make funny grimaces, flail your arms, protest and spit. Later on, you are quite happy to have eaten your carrot mush, which gives you such good coloring. And everybody stops in the street or on the tram to take a closer look at you. On such occasions you wear your fancy little jacket, the rose one, you know the one from "Aunt" Maxwell.

Yes, now and then we leave you alone. But we do not worry, for cousin Regina is right: you are such a good child. Aunt Gerda said the same. She took care of you when your father and mother had gone to visit Opa Brien in Westphalia. Just imagine: he lives on an old farmstead, almost as old as Germany. There are pigs, horses, cows, geese and chickens; dogs, apples, pears and plums. There is also much work, because all the animals want to live, too. Opa Brien said that we should greet you from him, which Mother did. You listened well and put on your serious face.

(An entry of October 30, 1949) There is a new contraption since a few days. Mother invented it: an anchored featherbed. A string is attached from one of its corners to the other, going under the mattress. The effect is as surprising as it is practical: little Cornelia can no longer kick up her legs to free herself. So shedding your featherbed had until then been an unfriendly act. But no longer, for it has gotten cold.

Let's put your "wanted" poster together. Age: nine months. Color hair: dark blond. Size: growing. Color eyes: brown spots around the pupil. Teeth: four. Digestion: regular, disregarding the potty. Special marks: a bandage around the lower arm, from spilling Father's coffee. Responding to the name "Van der Lubbe" (the dim-witted Dutchman who had set the *Reichstag* building on fire in 1933).

Good-bye, little Cornelia: I must return to the chronicle of both family and society.

It was in late 1948 or early 1949 when my father fell victim to the denazification process. He had begun to make a name for himself with his radio ministry, and he was the senior pastor in the large Protestant congregation in Coblence. Physically less than robust and a busy man, going on sixty, he was beginning again to "put some flesh on his ribs" -- now that plenty of food was on the minister's table.

A French colonel, in particular, kept pressing for his removal from ecclesiastical prominence. Superintendent Sachsse and the church authorities in Düsseldorf caved in, I do not know how easily. And so Father was transferred to the sizable parish of Engers "in the hinterland." Engers is a medieval town overlooking the Rhine River some ten miles north of Coblence. Belonging to the Diocese of Treves, Coblence and its surroundings were largely Catholic, but a substantial number of Protestants had filtered in since the acquisition of the Rhineland by Prussia in 1815; and even more since World War II and the refugee influx in its wake.

The manse in Engers was just that: a large, off-white, square three-story building in a park-like setting, looking down upon the generally placid river and the undulating countryside beyond. Full of energy, Father applied himself to both the parish chores and the extensive fruit and vegetable garden behind the house. He quickly increased its yield: an ingenious pole-and-water-spray contraption saw to that.

Soon, he acquired one of those miniscule BMWs, a 500-ccm job with a flat nose, four wheels and two tiny doors through which Father and Mother would squeeze themselves. The lively machine greatly decreased the physical effort of ministering to his flock in a ten-square mile parish. Father continued his radio ministry, rotating with other pastors; worked well with the Catholic priest and the townspeople; and served as chaplain to a large state-run rehabilitation center, housed in a once beautiful but now run-down Episcopal *Schloss*. Father never dwelt on his forcible transfer to Engers, at least not in our presence. Strange that such an outgoing and alert man should be so tight-lipped about his true feelings and loyalties. Or is it?

Brother Richard had gotten his degree, finished his internship at the Kemperhof hospital in Coblence and opened a practice in a new building not far from the parents' house. He, Gerda and their two all-German, blond and blue-eyed daughters, Regina and Claudia, lived on the second floor. Soon, Richard moved up the professional and social ladder: to Bad Ems, a famous spa fifteen miles east of Coblence. Prosperity and vacation pleasures were returning after the dismal years of the war and its aftermath. With them, professionals, from doctors to accountants, lawyers to business people, were beginning to make good money.

Into this early recovery period fell my friendship with Reinhard Hauschild. The Hauschilds were an old Coblence family. For many years before the war the elder Hauschild had been headwaiter at a renowned restaurant on Goebenplatz. Reinhard, a year older than I, had graduated from the Augusta *Gymnasium* in early 1939 and suffered the same brutal treatment as I at the hands of mean Labor Service leaders in Kommlingen. He became an artillerist, saw heavy action and was injured on the Russian front. When we met again in 1948 he was a starveling journalist in Offenbach near Frankfurt and an aspiring author. He had recently married a pretty blond physical therapist and freelance sculptor by the name of Irmtraud.

Tall, extrovert, articulate and solidly Christian Democrat -- he came from a very Catholic family -- Reinhard and I probably met at one of Hans Bellinghausen's parties. His sister would soon marry Dr. Bellinghausen. By then, Hans, one of the four "tradition operators" from the boot-camp days in Posen and a fellow POW in Crossville, Tennessee, was on his way to becoming a well-heeled internist in Coblence. He had recently acquired a fabulous, if somewhat damaged, house on Asterstein, the steep hill on the other side of the Rhine.

Reinhard and I had much in common: the war, the hungry years after it and the ardent hopes for a new Germany to rise from the ashes. But we were quite opposite in our political orientation, probably because of our different assessment of both National Socialism and Communism. Like almost all men who had fought on the eastern front and as an ardent admirer of Dr. Adenauer, he was convinced that the Russians were just waiting for an opportunity to attack the Western Allies in Germany; and their recent attempts at strangling West Berlin seemed to prove him right.

Like most Germans, he had seen the pictures of the atrocities committed. He condemned them. But he would not admit to others, nor even to himself, that all Germans bore some responsibility for their leaders' falsehood, folly and fury before and, especially, during the war. Reinhard was opposed to what was becoming an important notion and emotion at home and abroad: that of the Germans' "collective guilt." And he saw the measures taken by the West, and America in particular, to stir the Cold-War pot as quite justified, without admitting that such policies might thwart the eventual reunification of the two Germanys.

I had come out of the war chastened and deeply conscious of my part, albeit ever so small, in Hitler's rise to power and descent to slaughter, in which all Germans then of age share a measure of responsibility -- and hence shame. Not having been in Russia, I did not share the acute fear of most Germans that the "Russians were coming down the pike."

As soon as he could, probably in 1953, Reinhard joined the new (West) German *Bundeswehr* and eventually made it to colonel on the General Staff; specialty: *innere Führung* (literally, inner leadership; perhaps better, character formation). To be sure, this was after our emigration to the USA. But for all our common interests in politics, history and writing, we had already drifted apart by the time our young family left Germany: victims of our own perceptions, hopes and, thus, directions. Still, Reinhard and Irmtraud took wonderful care of little Irene in the spring of 1951.

Little Irene? Spring of 1951? Obviously, I have advanced too rapidly and must retrace my steps to 1949. So: back to the wooden family album and the entry dated January 19, 1950.

(On that day) all four of us -- how come four? But I will return to that matter later -- were at Aunt Gerda's house because Cousin Regina had her third birthday. You were ever so well behaved, Cornelia.

May I come back to this "all-four-of-us" business? Let's count: first, of course, there is you (Cornelia). Father must not be forgotten. He is number two. Remains Mother. She makes numbers three and four. How so? Well, I'll explain this when you are a little older. And there may be an illustration of who number four is.

(September 16, 1950) Actually, a new story should begin on August 29, that of Angelika Irene. But so it is: after the first child, parents tend to lose a little interest in the small happenings surrounding the second child. Let me try the middle road: we will add the story of Irene to yours, Cornelia; to be followed by other stories which may come later -- but hopefully not too soon! And then the stories of all our children will be woven together, all right?

Just now, you are helping Mother prepare "happa" for Irene. Meanwhile, she has begun to cry and cough. Whereupon Cornelia: "Titti!" Titti (the baby) lies in the crib in the kitchen. It is not easy in a two-room apartment to keep the two *Schreihälse* ("crow-throats") apart, so that one does not disturb the other.

Irene could be four weeks already if she had been on time. But women tend to be less than punctual. And so Irene was born on August 29,

1950, at 3:30 in the morning. She measured 21-1/2 inches and weighed in at six pounds. We seem to remember that Irene had a slightly larger mouth than Cornelia and that her head was not as elongated. Moreover, your parents do not get excited any more when Irene cries or spits during the night. With the second child, you know, things quiet down.

But we have just noticed that you are jealous of little Irene. When she smacked on her bottle you wanted to have "happa," too; and cried and carried on when you did not get it. That was not nice.

From now on when I write this chronicle I have to make clear to whom I am referring, because we have two little "worms" now, although the older one is already a real "worm."

Our Irene: she is no longer pale and frail. Her coloring is good, although her hair is sparse. She has full cheeks. She laughs, "talks" and shouts for joy: a truly sunny child. However, when "Nena" (Cornelia) throws a rubber ball into her carriage, Irene starts to cry -- as she does when she has terrible hunger. But Mother makes sure that she does not go hungry for long. Vegetable mush is part of the new diet for you, Irene; the one with carrots is spread all over your face, like freckles.

Actually, Irene, you have a good life. You have an almost new wicker baby carriage. You are privileged to sleep in the warm kitchen, even if you have to inhale the kitchen fumes. Because of you, Mother has to get up at six -- if she does.

(July 18, 1951) Now you are almost a year old, Irene. You have become a solid and jolly fellow, with blue eyes, seven little teeth and blond curly hair. Father calls you "Matzkowski" or "Mullewatz"; Mother gives you many tender names. You have become a real rascal, talk back and sway back and forth in your carriage, like your father was reported to have done in his mesh-wire children's bed. You stand on robust legs, and one does well to harness you. Soon, you will advance to the play pen. You balance your "pu" (bottle) like your elder sister who 'phoned Father today, saying, "good day, Papa."

Much has happened since my last report: move to Rödelheim, then to Bad Homburg; the parents' trip to Italy; the arrival of a maid; new furniture. And we are already a real family; each member is a piece of all. So it is. And so it should be.

Cornelia and Irene: this your story is ending. It is meant to be a present for Mother's birthday on October 12 (1951). Be always good to her and bring her as much happiness as you have in the past two years.

The years from 1949 to 1951 brought major changes at home and at work. From a couple, we became a family. The parents' life would revolve around the children, Cornelia and Irene. The little girls were gaining daily: weight, hair, teeth, talk, habits good and bad and, yes, personality.

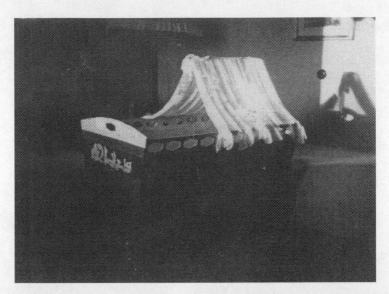

BMW, Engers, 1948

Uncle Hans (Ha) and Aunt Marguerite (Ma)

Reni's Baptism, Engers, 1950

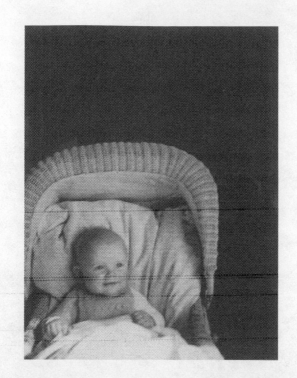

Irene

A CARE PACKAGE AND
PICKLED MUSHROOMS

Almost equally important changes were taking place on the job, although I am no longer sure in which exact sequence they occurred. It must have been in early 1949 when our simple office on Mainzerstrasse acquired a part-time "occupant."

A man of Father's age, of active disposition and with a bristly mustache, had found shelter in a corner of our office, on a donated bed and behind a donated blanket, near some relief supplies. Dr. Sachsse, the church leader in the French part of the Rhineland, must have asked Ray Maxwell to provide that shelter. Dr. Nölle, probably a lawyer, had been some high-level administrator in or for the many, and large, Protestant church institutions for the chronically ill, insane and handicapped. His task was to help them in matters of management and procurement -- now that the economy was beginning to stir and social services were returning to normal after years of danger, hunger and neglect. Outgoing Dr. Nölle was yet most discreet. By the time I got to the office well before Mr. Maxwell, our tenant had already left.

The larger context of work was also changing, though ponderously. The World Council's Division of Interchurch Aid was gradually assuming responsibility for refugee services in Germany, Austria and Italy, while that of the U.S.-based Church World Service for Displaced Persons was shrinking apace. And with Germany's accelerating recovery, relief moved toward the integration and rehabilitation of refugees.

Many kinds of people had been displaced by the war. They fell into two groups: former POWs and others from nations in eastern Europe who

103

did not want to return because their homelands were occupied by Soviet troops: Russians, Latvians, Estonians, Lithuanians, Poles, Rumanians and Hungarians; and German nationals or ethnic Germans from provinces occupied by Russia and Poland, as well as other east European countries where some of their families had lived and worked for centuries.

The former group, perhaps numbering 750,000, fell under the mandate of the International Refugee Organization. They lived mostly in camps. With the U.S. Displaced Persons' Act of 1951 and similar legislation in Canada, Australia and some Latin American countries, they had reason to expect visas fairly soon. Most wanted to go to the USA.

Most Hungarians and some Estonians and Rumanians, however, had a harder time finding international recognition and support because they had sided with Hitler Germany in the war; and it took a long time for the Hungarians to qualify for services in Germany and for emigration abroad.

The volume of relief supplies was shrinking, and CRALOG became somewhat of an anachronism, since German government and church authorities assumed ever more responsibilities, and discharged them well. Ray Maxwell became chairman of CRALOG in 1950 and was eventually awarded the *Verdienstkreuz* (merit cross) First Class.

However, the sharp dividing line between services for DPs, on one hand, and German refugees, as well as former POWs returning from Russia, on the other, got Ray and me into hot water soon, him more than me. Never mind the laudable World Council policy to help all refugees in need, staked out in two conferences in Imbshausen in what had become the *Land* (state) of Lower Saxony in 1950 and 1951.

A little background is necessary for the first crunching crisis. During the war some orphans and "planned" children of pure Aryan heritage -- blue-eyed, blond and strong -- had found shelter, education and opportunity in homes or institutions closely supervised by the Party and the state. This dubious enterprise in the creation of a master race was called *Lebensborn*, "fountain of life." With the end of the war some such children were given to or taken by German foster parents. The refugee offices of the occupation forces, though -- especially in the French Zone -- had other designs. If possible, they wanted to identify the non-German natural parents of such children and return the "orphans" to them.

Somehow, Ray Maxwell had heard of the plight of one well-intentioned German family near Bad Kreuznach who had cared for such a child for years. The French authorities threatened this couple to take the child away. Kind-hearted Ray helped to hide it. This did not sit well with the occupation department responsible for Displaced Persons in Rastatt. The ranking official there was a Jewish lady of Polish background who had advanced to such prominence in the occupation government. Ray was questioned and, as far as I know, yielded no information on the child's whereabouts. But a report about "obstructing justice" was sent to the World Council. Nothing came of it, but Ray's normally good relationships with the French authorities suffered a serious blemish.

At that time our office was still distributing CARE packages. They went to returning German POWs, in terrible shape after years of deprivation in Russia, and to Displaced Persons in the French-Zone camps, including some clergymen as poor as church mice. I helped compile lists and got the packages dispatched.

Little did I know, nor probably did Ray, that Church World Service had made an agreement with both CARE and the Tolstoy Foundation. The latter cared exclusively for Russian DPs. The package allocation for CWS was to include a share for such persons. I proceeded merrily with my distribution when, out of nowhere, an elderly woman -- "lady" seemed too elevated a term -- emerged to challenge Ray's and my package release.

Her name was Tatiana Schaufus. She was the senior Tolstoy Foundation representative in Germany. Around sixty and an American without traceable accent, she looked and acted the part of a heavy. Her bulging body had been pressed into an American uniform. Her tough-looking face showed some probably unwanted hair. In general, to call her an ugly woman would be both justified and impolite.

Well ... "Where," bellowed Mrs. Schaufus, "are 'my' CARE packages?" She explained her right to them in no uncertain terms. Ray cabled New York. And I sent some two dozen CARE packages, very quickly, to DPs named by her. Years later, when I worked in the Immigration Services of CWS in New York, "good old" Tatiana, under the benign but alert supervision of Countess Tolstoy herself, equally old and ugly, would on occasion sit with me in inter-agency meetings -- keeping, what seemed to me, a cold eye on me. I reciprocated with solicitous courtesy.

CARE packages. A Christmas party in a German relocation center near Bad Kreuznach. Honored guests. POWs just back from Russia, at long last. There was no light in their eyes, I said in a short essay which I wrote about the event. Briefly, I dwelt on the contrast in appearance and demeanor between the honored guests and the POWs.

... There was one POW's face, right between those of the pastors at my table. Did I say, face? Yes, it was a face -- but the eyes were dead. There was no more light in them, no Christmas lights. The face had been burnt out. This face had no soul, no chords to give an echo. Over there, near the Christmas tree, under short-clipped hair, the same dead eyes.

All of a sudden, I felt chilly. Was there a draft in the room? It felt as though the door had swung wide open and a Siberian wind had blown snow, ice and cold into the festive room, and all the miseries of our prisoners in Russia's desolate plains of winter. Did the candles not flicker?

(Later) ... I saw a prisoner who was about to open his CARE package. He was young. His hair was cut short. In his eyes there was something of the endless plains of Russia; but no light was there, none of the beaming happiness which might have been expected. He was too weak to break the metal bands of his CARE package, and I helped him. I felt his hands tremble with the effort.

I spread the cans and bags on his bed: flour, meat, margarine, chocolate and all the other beautiful things which, no doubt, he had not seen for years. He stared at them. He did not ask what the cans contained. He just stared and breathed heavily from the effort of opening the package and also perhaps from hurrying up the stairs. I explained the contents of the cans. He did not say a word. He stood and stared; not even a "thank-you." Then he took one of the cans and looked at it from all sides, as a child might look at his new toy: in silent admiration.

When we shook hands I felt again how weak his were. When he said goodbye, it must have been in such a low voice that I do not remember it. The last thing I saw when I left him was that he had picked up a can and seemed to meditate on words his lips tried to spell: "whole powdered milk."

Thus a CARE package came to a former prisoner of war.

Our work for Displaced Persons in the French Zone included the pastoral care for their clergy. There were some twenty of them, mostly Russian Orthodox. The latter looked the part: bearded, friendly, with a smattering of German, living in great simplicity. Ray visited them regularly and saw to their special needs. They included a steady supply of communion wine. I remember one such visit to an elderly priest near Mainz.

He greeted us at the door, embracing and kissing us on the cheek. He had borrowed two chairs for us to sit on in his cubicle, while he sat on the bed. The formalities over, he slowly bent down, reached under his bed, pulled out a large dusty jar with what looked like greenish pickles and mushrooms. He explained in pidgin German that, in honor of his visitors, he would open the jar to serve us this delicacy, which must have waited for the occasion for months, even years.

Now, Ray Maxwell for all his wonderfully patient and pastoral qualities, was not known for a strong stomach. Our host, though, insisted that we partake of his cherished treasure, those slightly moldy gray-green mushrooms. I rose to the task; Ray, turning pale, for no more than a bite. "They are excellent!"

WORK: WIDENING VISTAS

In these years of change, admittedly from a distance and second-hand, I got to know some of the main actors in the web of Church World Service and World Council of Churches activities in Germany. Perhaps Fred Ramsey should be mentioned first. It must have been in the winter of 1948-49 when he showed his rugged face and dreaded business acumen in Coblence. Indeed, he had been sent by CWS New York as a special envoy to assess the directions of relief, refugee and rehabilitation work and, more particularly, the place and prominence of that oh so different World Council of Churches, which was coming more and more into play.

Fred Ramsey was a successful businessman. He looked the part. Church organizations sometimes rely on such lay leaders to help -- or hinder -- them with strong management and tough decisions, top personnel changes often in their wake. I do not remember that Fred Ramsey made any lasting impact, but his arrival was preceded by much apprehension and even fear, especially in Munich-Pasing. The headquarters of the International Refugee Organization was there, as was that of CWS. A 300-pounder, reported to be fond of drink and high living, was in charge of a large DP resettlement and welfare operation. There were six or eight field offices, including a few in Austria; and an expatriate staff of at least a dozen men and women. Soon, the CWS director in Munich and the senior welfare administrator were gone.

A new World Council appointee, representing its Division of Interchurch Aid, settled down in a large requisitioned villa on the edge of a park in the famous spa of Bad Homburg, some twenty miles north of Frankfurt. Dean Høgsbro was a handsome and crusty Dane; his assistant a blond and tall lady, Bodil Jensen, also from Denmark. Dean Høgsbro meant business:

he expected regular reports, including those financial; he traveled around; he obviously had the confidence of the higher-ups in Geneva.

As the World Council's role in Germany gained leadership, focus and direction, I heard it said -- though perhaps not meant for the ears of some German underling -- that while the British and the Dutch had lost their empires they had won the World Council of Churches! At that time, its General Secretary was William Visser t'Hooft, a Dutch pastor of stellar convictions, skills and theology. I would see him later when I worked in Geneva in the seventies: retired, he yet would not miss the obligatory tea-time break -- see empires -- sitting by himself or occasionally inviting younger colleagues to keep him company. I would say even then that his craggy face looked like that of one of those wooden nutcrackers!

The World Council's most important division, that of Interchurch Aid, was run by a Scottish Presbyterian, Robert Mackie. In 1950 he must have been in his mid-fifties. I did not get to know him personally until the mid-sixties on the occasion of a WCC Central Committee meeting in Rochester, NY. Dr. Mackie, for his elevated position, competence and wonderful wit, yet deeply cared for people. Of him it was said in the late forties that he would sit up all night on the train to save the churches' money. He also had a glass eye, and there was a constant twinkle about his eyes and brows.

During that Rochester meeting -- I was only a mid-level staffer in one of CWS' member agencies -- he had, exhausted, retired to a sofa in a quiet corner when I chanced by. He called me to sit with him and chatted with me about CWS, my work and life in the USA, his "twinkling" eye fastened on me with interest. No wonder that Dr. Mackie was both respected and loved.

It is conceivable that U.S. denominational hierarchies placed some of their best people with either Church World Service or, if possible, with the World Council of Churches. It is no less conceivable that some of their not-so-good leaders were so "compensated" for not making bishop or general secretary in their own churches! At any rate, to invigorate the refugee service leadership in Europe, a U.S. Congregational minister by the name of Edgar Chandler made his appearance in Geneva and Germany by early 1950.

Edgar with his handsome face, bushy brows and engaging laughter was most energetic. He traveled much -- with an old bulging *Brieftasche* (attaché case) of German make and proportions. It was brimful with papers. But Dr. Chandler never had to search for the one needed. I never found out, though I tried, how so swiftly and unerringly he could do that. Anyhow, he organized and expanded the World Council's refugee service, especially that for resettlement, and harnessed the operation of a dozen or so field offices in all western zones of occupation in Germany, Austria and Italy.

An early acquisition of the World Council of Churches, perhaps immediately after the war when it was still in process of formation, was a Welsh Congregationalist. Compared to the rather regular ways of Mackie and Chandler, his were noticeably eccentric.

Elfan Rees was in his late fifties. He sported fine jackets of Scottish tweed and patterns and a reddish mustache, ends up. A large white handkerchief was hidden in his sleeve while a budding rose adorned his lapel. A small phial with water kept it fresh. He was a brilliant speaker and a writer no less. It was said that he was the principal thinker and writer behind the United Nations' charter. It is believable. But an administrator he was not; and around 1949 he thus moved from the refugee service directorship to be an advisor on refugee affairs. He wrote a much read and acclaimed booklet entitled *The Century of the Homeless Man*, a powerful challenge to churches and governments alike, pleading the cause of refugees.

I did not know him personally then, although I had heard him speak eloquently at one of the Imbshausen conferences. But I had to cope with the fact that on one of his field trips in the French Alsace he had to buy a new tire. He paid for it in German Marks or Swiss Franks -- whichever -- and we had to reimburse him. The transaction became a complicated international currency exchange which I did not know how to enter in our books!

Of Dr. Rees it was reported that once when he was a panelist at a large international gathering and was called upon by some cheerful and energetic chairwoman to be the first to introduce himself, he said: "Ma'am Chairman, at this time of the day" -- it was about ten A.M. -- "I could not possibly tell who I am!" Long retired, he and Mrs. Rees were walking along the main street in the old town of Geneva when Heidi and I chanced upon them. He stopped us, chatted amiably, called me "Gerhard" and seemed to be quite familiar with my work on behalf of refugees in Germany and the USA decades earlier. Eccentric, surely; but likable, eminently.

Although British too, Frank Northam, a Methodist, was altogether different. Before the war he had been a chartered accountant for a British firm in Berlin. His German and French were fluent if you disregard his English accent in either. From at least 1947 on he was the Council's chief financial and administrative officer. Tall, handsome, knowledgeable far beyond accountancy and a genius in it, he became my mentor in setting up an accounting system in Germany. With the advice and cooperation of a private Frankfurt bank, he realized substantial *Deutschmark* resources at advantageous rates to finance WCC's operations.

In the confused and corrupt waning days of the IRO and CWS in Munich-Pasing -- it must have been in early December, 1951 -- he and I spent several cold and miserable days in the former caserns in Pasing: checking and researching accounts, trying to balance books hopelessly in arrears, upbraiding remaining staff about underhanded sales of equipment and vehicles and paying expatriate staff, some of whom had several months of salary coming to them. Frank was a firm, fair, patient and brilliant manager in the midst of a hopeless situation and among demoralized workers. He became both idol and friend.

But I have hurried ahead to make Frank come alive. I must return to the changing WCC Displaced Persons' program in Germany a year or two earlier. Dr. Rees in Geneva was not the only eccentric. Some were closer by. But they did not gain contours, faces and voices until the Maxwells and the office had actually moved to Bad Homburg to occupy that handsome and large turn-of-the-century villa. That must have been in the fall of 1950.

While still in Coblence and perhaps not unrelated to Ray's controversy about the *Lebensborn* child, our two-man team was augmented by a social worker from Geneva, Loïs Meyhoffer. She was around thirty, wore glasses and was a pleasant, even charming, lady. She did not drive. So a driver was hired. He came in the form of a forty-year old Bavarian transplant by the name of Wältl. He lived a few miles up the Moselle River, was married and had a small child. He was as reliable as he was competent. He took care of a couple of Volkswagens which had come down to our office via the IRO in-process-of-demise.

It was Loïs' task to assess and ameliorate the needs of Displaced Persons in the French Zone, especially those of their clergy. She spoke excellent English -- of the British kind -- and good German. She traveled much and worked hard to be a reassuring presence and advocate with the authorities, French and German, for those forlorn strangers in a country that was "finding itself" with ample energy and assertiveness, and rapid economic progress. But it was hard to integrate mostly Russian DPs who preferred to emigrate. Most still lived in camps and could not possibly forget what suffering the "master race" had wrought upon them. However, for many of them, the less fit and daring, emigration to North America or Australia presented almost equal obstacles.

A conference in Königsfeld in the Black Forest comes to mind. The site, a *Brüdergemeine* (Moravian) church and retreat place, was carefully chosen to provide a peaceful setting and spiritual atmosphere for some twenty clergy to pray, sing, ponder their needs and what WCC could do to minister to them and their dispersed flocks. The Russians: all properly bearded, robed and marvelous singers.

Some time earlier, and for several months, Ray Maxwell and I had worked on an altogether different kind of endeavor for clergymen. In this, an American Congregational minister and New Englander of Ray's age was his partner. Howard Schomer was soft-spoken, lean and bilingual. For years he had been the chaplain at an American-sponsored college at Chambon-sur-Lignon in France. A pastors' exchange between Protestant French and German clergy was arranged; the latter to spend two weeks at a retreat in Chambon with their French counterparts.

Count Yorck von Wartenburg, from a famous Prussian family and remarkable in his own right for his resistance to Hitler, a man of vision and connections, helped Ray and Howard to open doors and overcome enmity long before, on a more public and prominent level, Konrad Adenauer and Charles De Gaulle would do so. Even so stiff and anti-German a man as Géneral Koenig -- the defender of Bir Hacheim during the Battle of Tobruk in 1942 and the top French representative in their zone of occupation -- paid a grudging compliment to such novel and revolutionary idea and practice. For once the Church was in the lead, reconciling.

Conference with Russian-Orthodox Clergy, Königsfeld, Black Forest 1952

BAD HOMBURG

From childhood on, I had suffered from a disease the Germans call *Fernweh*: a longing for places distant, even exotic; to be where one is not. It was therefore not surprising that the confined years of the war and the miserable ones in its wake would heighten my desire to "go south," at least to the Italy I had come to know and love -- just as soon as frontiers opened again and transport and a bit of money were available. But the children were small in June 1951; in fact, Irene was a mere nine months old. So what!

She was parked with the Hauschilds in Offenbach, recently married; and Irmtraud turned out to be an excellent substitute mother. Cornelia stayed with her Oma in Engers. And off we went, Heidi and I, caps, goggles and an old coverall -- and much too much luggage. Part of it would be shed soon, when we visited my former driver in Offenburg, lightening our 125-ccm NSU and our own discomfort.

It felt good to be "free" and young, to head toward the sun, to cross frontiers and, the first night, to stop at a large villa sitting in a lovely park on Lake Zurich. "Aunt" Emma was in her late seventies then: a matronal, alert and charming woman. I believe that she was related to the Morfs, partners of Grandfather Grunwald in Kobe, Japan, in the eighteen-eighties and -nineties. Heidi and I had a splendid room, delicious meals and a short walk along the pretty lakeshore. A band of medieval burghers marched by, to the accompaniment of drums and fifes. It happened to be the time for the *Sechserläuten*, the evening vesper bells and the mounting of the guard. Blessed, peaceful Switzerland! "Aunt" Emma gave us fifty Swiss Francs, a substantial sum in view of our meager travel "kitty."

The trip was one continuous adventure and wonder: Florence, Siena, soaking wet from steady rain around hill-crest Radicófani in Tuscany, Rome, Naples, Capri, the Amalfi Drive, Pompeii and Mount Vesuvius. Disaster struck on May Day, May 1, a holiday in an Italy ruled by Socialists and Communists. The ballbearing in the rear wheel gave out. We pushed the bike a couple of miles along the suddenly hot *Autostrada* in the direction of Naples.

A filling station, open! The attendant had been a soldier in North Africa; a quick friendship. He also was an excellent mechanic. No charge. Long live comradeship! And off, on our way to the great city and, after some searching for cheap quarters, to a neglected apartment above a large courtyard owned by an engineer whose only outfit seemed to be his pajamas! After exploring and enjoying Naples the next day was spent near Pozzuoli. During the night following we came to realize, too late, that our "hotel" was probably a bordello!

And back north across the still-snowcapped Abruzzi, in sight of the Gran Sasso where -- how long ago? -- Mussolini had been "rescued" by German paratroopers; along the Adriatic coast, across the Brenner Pass and back home through Austria and southern Germany. Quickly, we were reunited with our children who seemed to appreciate our return with beaming faces.

Another such trip, though with much less luggage, in the early summer of 1952: across the western Alps to Geneva, along the Route Napoléon to the French Riviera and through northern Italy. It is not clear whether Heidi was actually comfortable on the rear seat. But she was game. And we had another long-delayed wedding trip.

Of course, that tireless NSU "horse" was not just for vacation journeys. In early 1950 Ray Maxwell was promoted to take Dean Høgsbro's place but not before another protégé of the dean had made his appearance as an unnecessary associate. Pastor Sølling was handsome in a bland way, a tall and blond Nordic figure utterly lacking the dean's and perhaps other Danes' energy. However, he smoked cigars and seemed to drink a bit. While his half-hearted efforts to strengthen our team were close to nil and he got on Ray's nerves, he did manage to fall in love with the dean's assistant and, before long, marry her. (I met Bodil Jensen-Sølling in 1995 when she represented Danchurchaid at a New York meeting. We did not talk about Mr. Sølling.)

Until an apartment could be found in or around Bad Homburg -- they were hard to come by -- I would live with the Maxwell family and their maid in that lovely villa. My NSU facilitated the commute from and to Arenberg. The 50-mile trip through the Westerwald and the Taunus became a routine Friday evening and early Monday morning ride. It also became a hazardous affair in fog, snow and ice. But the little silvery-and-blue thing never failed me.

In the villa, though, trouble was brewing just below the surface. No sooner had the Maxwells moved than Ilse insisted on having a full-time live-in maid. Her station simply required that. I partook of the meals, had a small room in the third-floor attic and used the bathroom three stairs down. On occasion, Hilde, the maid -- a wonderful, forbearing and hard-working 25-year-old East Prussian refugee -- had a day off, and Mrs. Maxwell had to cook. She hated it and, most of all, disliked cooking for me as well. One morning, I recall, she made scrambled eggs, and a few shells came with them. It triggered an outburst on her part which Ray, always patient, gentle and surely embarrassed, tried to squash.

Generally, he had a hard time with his beautiful, uppity and demanding wife. One perennial problem was Sigurd, Ilse's son by her former marriage, about eight by then and adopted by Ray. He was the prototype of a German spoilt brat who, with his mother's apparent approval, went out of his way to make his father, the maid and me miserable. Understandably, he was enamored with my motorbike and enjoyed climbing on it -- toppling it once. He did not hurt himself, but I forbade him to go near the thing again. Sigurd was more than a mere brat; he was mean-spirited.

Soon, Mrs. Maxwell needed a second maid, and another young refugee woman joined Hilde. Whenever visitors of consequence showed up, Ilse would play every bit of the lady of the house with superb meals -- and charm slightly overworked. Little wonder that Hilde and her helper were busy to the point of exhaustion. Keeping the books, I knew that Ilse's ménage, most of it reimbursed, was a rather hefty item in our financial reports to Geneva. For all the contretemps behind the façade and social polish of the villa, Ray's and my relationship remained strong and trusting, perhaps yet another reason for Mrs. Maxwell's and my mutual dislike.

By then I was paid a regular *Deutschmark* salary, though without benefits, from what was called "occupation costs," presumably furnished by the new more affluent German government for the presence of both military units and civilian "hangers-on," such as international organizations. I believe that my monthly wage was in the DM 350 range (about $80). This was quite sufficient, especially since I did not eat at home during the week.

Already in the last summer in Coblence, 1950, I had resumed playing tennis. Soccer belonged to the past, although I helped the SV Weilburg one year, for DM 20 ($5) a clip and as a commuter from Arenberg, to stay in the top regional league. An important "friendship" match between Weilburg and arch-rival Löhnberg held high expectations for the thousand-or-so spectators. I suffered a serious ankle injury and had to be taken off the field on a stretcher. Weilburg lost 0:3. For Mother, in particular, soccer became the worst of sports of which, in general, she did not have a clue!

In tennis, though, it was fun to trounce the top players in Coblence who had survived the war, even though our school-time courts had fallen victim to the bomb carpets in 1944. At the end of the 1951 season I became city champion. My opponent was a French lieutenant, son of a general later stationed in Algeria and sacked by De Gaulle for opposing the president's painful peace overtures. The general himself handed me the trophy, a silver chalice.

After our move to Bad Homburg, the handsome tennis clubhouse, bordering a large park, and the impeccable courts became the scene of my renewed efforts. Dr. Zur, a suave "middle-aged" doctor catering to the needs, perceived or real, of an increasingly affluent clientele, and a young strapping fellow soon fell victim to this social outsider; as did Hannes Braun, a good-looking "nouveau riche" who was making fast bucks with a new express bus connection between Bad Homburg and Frankfurt, pretty stewardesses the principal asset. Already, the once downtrodden Germans had come a long way toward means, recognition, glamour and even opulence.

Some of the building and re-building proceeding at a frantic pace was for refugees, bombed-out citizens and others disadvantaged. Ray Maxwell exercised some pull with Evangelisches Hilfswerk and its allied "social" building projects. A small apartment in Rödelheim, fifteen miles east of Bad Homburg, was assigned to us. But then, the second floor of a "settler's" house for refugees came free on the outskirts of Bad Homburg. It was built from *Lastenausgleich* (equalization of burdens) funds, an important process integral to the 1948 currency reform. It was far from finished, at 8 Hasselmannstrasse.

Time to move. It must have been in early 1951. We occupied the second floor of half of a two-family house. The Dahnkes on the ground floor were refugees from East Prussia, like Heidi. He was a tall rough-and-ready painter, now making good money and spending long weekend hours on improving his own house and access to it.

Mrs. Dahnke was on the chubby side, flax-blond and outgoing. Daughter Heike, a year older and much bigger than Cornelia, turned out to be a venturesome youngster with a steady snot-nose. Quickly, Connie would imitate her in her own exploits in garden, field and "street," dirty to the gills!

We had a small kitchen-living room, a tiny bathroom with shower and two medium-size bedrooms. The staircase had no railing yet; much interior work still needed doing. But with Heidi's indefatigable efforts and cleanliness, by spring we were quite comfortable in our new home. And the long-distance motorbike commutation was a matter of history.

By then, Bad Homburg had returned to its reputation as a spa. There were the serene *Kurpark*, the ducal castle, re-built and re-stocked stores, sidewalk cafés and plenty of patrons to match -- and create -- the rising living standard and pretty sights. One of the ministers in town was Uncle Paul, second son of Oma's brother Paul. He taught me the "match-and-stubble" trick, a favorite with small children ever since. He was the older brother to Uncle "Ha" and Aunt "Ma" in Weilburg. We visited Uncle Paul's family a couple of times. He died shortly after our emigration, leaving behind his wife with six children, one of them retarded.

Household help was still obtainable. We had heard, I believe from Cousin Lili, that *Fräulein* Barth, before the war housekeeper of Uncle Adolf in Weilmünster, had survived the war. She must have been in her early sixties then and lived nearby. We contacted her and were surprised that she did not respond to our offer to help Heidi with the chores. We heard a few months later that she had committed suicide just at the time of our invitation. Was she seriously ill? Was she in dire economic straits and all alone? We never found out.

In her stead came Lieselotte. She was about fifteen, scrawny and not so strong on hygiene. But in this, or any other, trait she was no match for the "lady of the house," who wanted her kids as neat as a pin. Good-natured, Lieselotte applied herself and became a pretty good junior nanny.

No sooner had we found our level on Hasselmannstrasse than, after careful evaluation with Horst and Christel, Heidi's sister, we offered our help to Horst to move to the Frankfurt area which promised gainful employment more readily than "end-of-the-line" Flensburg.

Oma Brien, Christel and Karin, her young child by a professional non-commissioned officer, had fled from Elbing in January 1945, the dreaded Russian armies advancing relentlessly. Eventually, they arrived near Flensburg where, later, Frieda Brien met and came to love a postal employee, Emil Ludwig, while her husband stayed a POW in Russia for at least four years. Edwin, Christel's husband, too, was taken prisoner by the Russians. He must have come home a year or two earlier than his father-in-law. At any rate, Christel's marriage did not last long; and after some off-and-on relationship with a Saxon by the name of Paul, she and Horst had found each other and married, probably in 1950.

Pleasant and funny Horst, blind in one eye, had begun his bank apprenticeship early in the war and, since 1945, had been living hand-to-mouth in Flensburg by repairing watches. He was naturally anxious to return to his profession. Quickly, he landed a job with his old bank, the Dresdner in Frankfurt. The Dahnkes were prevailed upon to rent him a room, where he stayed for a few months. Ray Maxwell, once again via Evangelisches Hilfswerk, helped Horst, soon to be joined by Christel, to find a half-house in a state-financed settlement in Frankfurt-Zeilsheim. There, they have "lived happily ever after."

As for Opa Brien, when he came home around 1950 and found his wife living with another man, he moved to Westphalia, worked on a large farm for a short year and then re-entered the postal service in Opladen, north of Cologne. Before long, he met and married a rather large and most pleasant fellow worker. They had two children: Gottfried, thin as a bean-pole, and Margrit, more than plump and like her mother. Around 1955 Opa Brien died from some painful kidney disease, probably the after-effect of his years of deprivation in Russian POW camps.

The story of the Lakows and the Briens was typical of that of thousands, even tens of thousands, of refugees from Germany's eastern provinces: skilled, motivated, industrious, relocated and trained, they became part of the driving energy behind the "German miracle" unfolding in the early fifties. For us, too, the year 1952 brought further progress.

But before I return to our life in Bad Homburg, to Hasselmannstrasse and our daughters' rapid growth, so enjoyable for them and their parents, a further look at the changing context of my work is in order. Once again, let me enliven it by describing some of the "character players" related to the World Council's refugee work in Germany. And "characters" they were.

By 1951 Bad Homburg had clearly become the "center" of representation for the World Council of Churches and its work for Displaced Persons in West Germany: Ray Maxwell its "director," I somewhat of a business manager. Beyond its oversight task for a dozen field offices, whose dual and often mutually exclusive functions were to integrate these refugees into the Germany economy and society, on one hand, or to facilitate their emigration, on the other, there were our own tasks: letters, accounts, telephone calls, reports.

Residual care for Russian and other Orthodox DPs, and their clergy, in the re-established *Land* (state) of Bavaria had fallen to an Anglican priest, Ben Dakin. He had his very own ways and seemed to resist, even resent, notions advanced by his fellow Anglican Ray Maxwell who, after all, was but an American Episcopalian. To Ray's relief, Mr. Dakin did not stay long.

In his place -- and, one must assume, with some hesitation on the part of superiors in Geneva -- came a Rumanian Orthodox layman, Mr. Gallin. He had the polished ways and gray-at-the-temples looks of a diplomat, which he had been in the service of the recently executed General Antonescu of "Iron Guard" infamy. At least, so went the scuttlebutt. Thus his work for the large majority of Russian DPs in his care was not without tension and frustration. Fortunately, a very energetic and competent German secretary made up for Mr. Gallin's somewhat tainted and detached "ministry."

At the end of the war some Displaced Persons had been stranded in Italy. They may have been auxiliaries to German troops or forced labor. A resettlement office in Rome cared for them. Growing numbers of Albanians, Yugoslavs and Bulgarians were "filtering" across the Adriatic Sea: mostly single men and, therefore, hard to resettle. Prince Encalichev, of ancient Russian aristocracy, was responsible for their welfare. Eventually, it turned out, that he was more interested in his own; and Frank Northam had to scramble to make up the $60,000 which had somehow disappeared from the Rome accounts.

Through my administrative and financial responsibilities, other expatriates could be seen or discerned, if from some distance. There was Arthur Wilde, a British ex-captain in the Hamburg-Wentorf office, less than a team player. There were Arthur Foster, Christopher King and Jim Atkinson, a very British triumvirate in Austria. The last-named -- tall, lanky, with an eagle's beak and a racy Jaguar -- while on a late-night trip to Geneva came down one of those winding roads and into a village. Out of breath and somewhat wild-eyed, but "cool under fire," he pulled up in front of a small police station to report in atrocious German that "some bandits up on the mountain have tried to stop and rob me. But, of course, I got away in my Jaguar." Alas, the very stolid Swiss-German *Gendarme* would not believe him: bandits in Switzerland?

Which strange story is perhaps not so far from the joke I must have heard around that time. Somewhere in the remote mountains of southern Yugoslavia: a few shepherds. They first notice and then observe a bunch of strangers, back-pack and all, working their way up to them. The shepherds: "Aren't you lost, foreigners?" "Lost perhaps, but foreigners, no. We are British!"

Perhaps the most important -- and most difficult -- field office in West Germany was that in the spa of Bad Salzuflen. It was responsible for the British Zone. Here, one should perhaps say, reigned David Paterson-Morgan, another Englishman -- see empire. In his late thirties and handsome in a stiff way, he had been a British policeman for a dozen years somewhere in the vast hinterland of India, the only white face among a few million brown people. P. M., as he was called, had his own ways and somewhat suspect direct lines to Geneva.

His deputy for resettlement was, if possible, even more British and a spitting likeness of Governor and Vice President Nelson Rockefeller -- had I known the latter in 1951. A young escapee from the 1917 Russian Revolution, Andy Mouravieff, of illustrious family history, was of medium build and manners ever so English, perhaps from having attended an exclusive "public" school in his adopted country. He made no bones about disliking Americans and distrusting Germans. That he had a stable of race horses could not be verified by my own eyes.

With our own emigration, I lost track of David Paterson-Morgan. But Andy Mouravieff "re-appeared" in the mid-fifties as the WCC representative in Brazil. There, he married his predecessor, a British lady, and continued to spice his correspondence about cases to be re-resettled from Brazil in the USA with unnecessarily unfriendly asides. Obviously, he made it hard for me to forget him.

And so in 1952, with much interesting and expanding work -- and the chores and joys of a young family's life -- spring turned into summer. My new "elevated" position bore unexpected fruits: the "CWS" personnel office in Munich, drawing on "occupation costs," reclassified my position; and I got DM 1,250 in retroactive salary, beyond the same very substantial monthly amount ($300).

After that second trip through southern France and northern Italy our NSU had some 70,000 miles on its back. With our sudden "affluence" I -- and I must confess, I alone -- made the decision to upgrade our means of transport to a 150-ccm "dual-piston" Puch, a blue 6-1/2 horse devil of an Austrian motorbike. It was driven for a few days before the family knew of it! Now and then, and off the beaten path to avoid the police, all four of us would take it for a short and slow spin: Heidi on the rear seat, Irene in her lap and Cornelia straddling the tank. A fine machine it was.

More consequential than my new "play machine" was the assessment of my long-term future with a foreign relief and refugee organization in a swiftly changing and ever more prosperous Germany. Sooner or later, surely, Displaced Persons would integrate as best they could or emigrate; and German refugees, already gainfully employed and decently housed, were on their own.

Return to university study to get a degree in philology or law? Mother was pleading for that. Seek an administrative or financial job in the burgeoning market place, building on my linguistic skills? Perhaps a career in the fledgling West German foreign service? After five years I had come to like working for an international outfit, even one church-related. Helping those in need while making a decent living through interesting work and in the company of interesting people: why not? Time for a decision seemed to draw near. And I knew that Heidi would wonderfully support me -- in whatever I chose.

This my inclination was also influenced by larger and more ethereal matters. I was unhappy with the thought of going back for more "wisdom" to largely over-aged and stale university professors. I was equally dismayed at national policies and politics which seemed to me to be left and warmed over from the failed Weimar Republic. But most of all, I was distraught by the constantly agitated fear that the Soviets were about to attack West Germany, thus conjuring up the "necessity" for arming it. Arming Germans again after their crushing defeat seven years earlier when that very defeat was to assure those same Germans, and the world at large, that their country be disarmed, dismantled and neutralized for good? My opposition to such rearmament, which incidentally preceded that of East

Germany by the Russians, came with the conviction that the longed-for German reunification would forever be out of the question.

Later on in my work in New York for refugee immigrants I would assert and define that in a person's decision to move from one country to another there were always push and pull factors. In the case of escapees, the very fear for their lives and freedom was a powerful push factor. But for most others not so compelled, unhappiness with or uncertainty about the circumstances in which the prospective migrant finds himself push; and he is pulled by what he mostly imagines are the opportunities in his new country. Clearly, I belonged to this second category.

From what I had seen of the United States, if from the windows of a guarded railroad coach or from behind barbed wire, here was a vast and varied country with tall opportunities for the bright, healthy and industrious. Here was a fresher, newer and less "class-ridden" and history-burdened society. Of course, I did not know that the USA was a land of opportunity rather than one of welcome. Thus, pushed by presumed constraints in Germany, pulled by beckoning opportunities in America and, no doubt, infused by my peculiar *Fernweh*, I leaned more and more toward emigration.

So why not apply for visas to the USA, using my second-hand connections in New York? Long forms were filled out. On them I answered the question about who paid for a possible earlier passage with: "I do not know who paid for it; whether it was the German or the American government!" The denazification certificate as a "pardoned youthful offender" was attached to our application. But a sponsor was needed. Who in CWS could help us with one?

The top man in New York, I found out later, was called "Executive Director." Wynn Fairfield was a former Congregational missionary to China. When I got to know him in January 1953, he turned out to be most competent and caring. Closer to Ray Maxwell, though, was the number-two man, a Baptist minister by the name of Wayland Zwayer, who had visited Bad Homburg once or twice. He was also the liaison man with the World Council of Churches. Naturally, I consulted with Ray regarding my plans. Sorry to lose me, he yet supported them. That support took the form of a letter to Roland Elliott.

Mr. Elliott was the director of the CWS Immigration Services, by far the largest unit. Ray did not know him personally. Yes, replied Mr. Elliott, he needed a financial assistant, mostly to collect a large number of accounts receivable for the inland transportation and other incidental costs of many of the 30,000 Displaced Persons who had arrived in the USA on CWS sponsorships between 1950 and 1952. Thus, and most convincingly, CWS itself became my sponsor and, sooner than expected, my employer as well.

While this emigration process moved forward rather rapidly, Ray had a new secretary assigned to him: a very British lady, Gwen Baer. She was in her early forties and was married to a German or DP architect in Bad Homburg. A pleasant and skilled local woman, with good English, was also hired to take care of the books once I left.

Just then, WCC was in the process of setting up a new accounting system for its world-wide refugee field offices. A young Geneva accountant or banker, Pierre Barrelet, who worked under Frank Northam, would help our office with that. Meanwhile, after a pro-forma interview with a consular officer in Frankfurt, our immigration visas were issued and stamped into our new passports: one for me and one for Heidi and the children. It all went so quickly. The momentum overtook us.

A cheerful, knowledgeable and personable Pierre Barrelet arrived in November 1952. Soon, he was like a family friend. The new accounting system was manual: with lined sheets for each account, from those for bank balances to that for currency exchanges to an increased number of expense accounts, in Bad Homburg and each field office. A control ledger recorded all entries, moving each new one forward by one line. A relatively simple affair; and *Fräulein* Rudek and I were eager learners. Monthly reports were then sent to Geneva.

125

"Aunt" Emma's Villa, Zürich

Farewell from Parents, Emmelshausen December 1952

All Aboard, S.S. Italia

January 1953

THE BIG CITY

Fall turned into winter. Purchases were made for all of us, for we had no idea about shopping in the USA. Heidi insisted on my getting an "employer's" hat; that is one with the rim up! Once we got to the USA, it was soon discarded. The Puch motorbike was sold, with more than a touch of sadness.

Relatives were visited. Father supported our decision manfully, suppressing his sorrow at seeing us go. Mother had a hard time with it all. Cornelia and Irene sailed through these commotions and emotions with cheer and nonchalance.

The World Council provided us with a travel loan, as it did for many other migrants. CWS would collect it; indeed, it would be my responsibility to collect it on behalf of WCC. Christmas came and went. What would Christmases be like in distant New York? The Lakows and we celebrated New Year's Eve at the Hotel zur Krone in Weilburg, recently vacated by its American soldier patrons.

We had decided that I would fly ahead on January 6, 1953. Heidi and the girls were to follow by ship a good week later. In this way, an apartment could be found and furniture bought in good time. Ray Maxwell permitted Pierre Barrelet to drive me to the Frankfurt airport, and the family all the way to Bremerhaven. Not a hitch in so momentous a change.

Roland and Florence Elliott were at Idlewild airport, as was a Latvian lady, a CWS employee responsible for meeting immigrants at airports and piers. Mr. Elliott, as I would call him for many months, was friendly and solicitous; a big-boned man with glasses and fading reddish hair. Mrs. Elliott, as all of us would call her until we lost track of her after Roland's death in 1959, was a slight, bespectacled and sharp lady. The Elliotts were to treat our whole family with parent-like affection and understanding.

As CWS Immigration-Services director, Roland was well known to the passport-control and customs officials. The four of us made our way into town in a taxi. Did I stay with the Elliotts on West 103rd Street for a couple days? On the first weekend in New York, then, and armed with a subway map, I went looking for an apartment.

What a smooth way to go from one country and continent to another! I had left work in Bad Homburg on a Tuesday. On Wednesday I started working for the same organization in New York. As easy as that.

Mr. Strauss -- he would probably have objected to *Herr* Strauss -- came from Aachen (Aix-la-Chapelle), was an émigré from Hitler Germany and owned a small real-estate office on Queens Boulevard. Attracted by the large green park areas in that part of Queens, as shown on my map, I drifted into his office. He had several two-bedroom apartments for rent. Yes, he would show them to me.

And so, within the hour, our family found reasonable shelter not far from the Grand Union supermarket on Union Boulevard in Kew Garden Heights, half a mile from the nearest subway stop on the IND line. Basic furniture and furnishings? Easy to come by. The apartment and I were ready for the arrival of Heidi and the girls.

They arrived around January 25 at a Hoboken pier. Again, the Elliotts were present to welcome them, through this interpreter. Smiles all around. And again, Roland shepherded us quickly by the authorities, except that, for an unusually long time, the Immigration and Naturalization Service inspector kept comparing the girls' passport pictures, six months old, with the little girls standing in front of him: he needed to make sure that we did not smuggle in some very young "illegals."

In a little piece I wrote on January 27, 1953 -- one day after my thirty-first birthday -- I conveyed "impressions of an immigrant" under the heading *New York Is a Big Place*. With it, I will conclude this chronicle.

> A man walks ahead of me: an old man, for the hair under his crumpled hat is white. A cold wind seizes pedestrians at the street corners. From the grids above the subways and the sewer lids emerges breath-like steam, instantly dissolved by the wind.
>
> The man has stopped. As I pass him I can take a closer look: yes, he has white hair and a white beard, and eyes tired and sad. He does

not look at me. He wears a large coat over his jacket, and over that, a tattered overcoat.

Now, he searches in his pockets with trembling and clammy hands. His hands hold a few cigarettes. Two or three fall down; and I ask myself whether he has noticed it. Yes, he bends down slowly, like old people are wont to; and he seems to mutter a few words. But in the wind and the noise of passing cars I cannot hear what he says. He has picked up all cigarettes, stands still and starts again to rummage in his multiple pockets.

I walk on, through the strange large city. When I turn around one more time at the next street corner, he still stands there, the old man.

In one of the streets between the rows of towering buildings made of dark stone; at night, a thousand lights, the moving reflections of lit billboards, cars and wet asphalt; in one of those endless straight streets, a gorge cut into sky-high walls under the sky's narrow strip, a strip bright from the reflection of the city's million lights: --

Cars chase cars. Suddenly, all of them stop, silently or with a slight sigh, catch their breath. Along the street, I see but red traffic lights, ten, fifteen, twenty. The avenues pause. But already, the swarm of cars comes from the side streets. Having rested for a minute, they must now seize their moment of movement.

And all about, the hurrying pedestrians. Among them is a stranger who listens to the breath of the strange city. The stranger is I.

Already, I can sleep in the subway, because I know that I am sitting in the F-Express which careens down Sixth Avenue and stops near the office on East 23rd Street.

Late one evening: few people on the subway. It hurries along, droning and rattling. The passengers are tired from the long workday, but almost all of them are reading papers, which in this county are as large as tablecloths and as thick as books. A few have dozed off only to jerk awake when the train suddenly brakes or stops.

The door from the next cars opens during the ride and a black man appears: in small steps, his head tilted backwards and sideways a bit as if listening to the train's rattle and roar. While he is putting one foot in front of the other, groping his way with legs slightly apart, he keeps knocking on the floor with his cane, rhythmically and fast: a begging beat. And so he stomps by and keeps his cane knocking the floor. There is a round white handle to the cane. He knocks and knocks.

But nobody looks up, nobody seems to hear the knocking -- yet I still remember the rhythmic sound.

There are trees in New York too, even in Manhattan. And birds. On this wet and gray day, warm like a day in March, I heard them sing in the trees on Washington Square.

The trees are small and dainty, almost like a breath drawn with tender strokes against the massive giants of stone. Those giants seem to squash the trees. Still, I heard the birds sing in the trees on the square.

Near the piers, suddenly, I saw a dead pigeon lie in the street: on his back, his head turned sideways a bit and his delicate little feet stretched up. Quickly, I walked away and past hangars, trailer-trucks and warehouses. Far away, in the mist and the gray of the waning day: the foghorns of ships.

When one is new and strange to the Big City one longs for Germany. One longs for a meal in a German restaurant. Here, one plunks oneself down on a stool at the counter, hat and coat left on, orders, gulps down the food, slides off the stool while the next one stands behind it, waiting, pays; and one has lunched.

Yes, one longs for a cup of coffee "without footbath," for a waiter who truly waits on you and reads your lips for every possible wish.

One longs for German dance music and for that orderly office in Germany. Here, the heat in the apartments and offices is suffocating. No wonder that folks are always drinking water: with their coffee, at lunch-time, with a sandwich, even with ice cream.

This was the worst in the first few days: the meals and the heat in the office.

These first impressions, seizing me with their rough and strange ways, are getting blurred. I should have written them down right away. But there was simply too much that was new, that confuses, that blunts.

I have a job, an apartment. At noontime I sit on a stool at the counter, wolf down my meal, leaving my hat on. The Big City has engulfed me with its haste, its noise and its very breath.

In the morning I squeeze myself into the subway car, rush up from the underground platform, turn on the neon light in my dingy office, work, live -- live ever further away from Germany. And last night, sitting at the counter, I caught myself staring at the television screen, heard myself laugh at the jokes on that milky screen, just like the others sitting on their stools.

New York is a big city: with subways, many people in them -- almost three million using them each day -- and many cars and billboards, and with television. Yet a Big City with trees, even birds; an old man, a blind black man and -- Bobby.

Bobby is the little fellow who helped me today to carry the grocery bags home from the supermarket around the corner. It stormed and rained. Once already, I had put down the bags. Then my hat flew off. I had to put them down again to retrieve that fine hat bought against my better judgment.

Bobby is a swift little guy with an open face, bright eyes and a turned-up nose. He talked to me from behind: "Mister, can I help you?"

And when we had gotten all food bags into our apartment -- meanwhile, he had suggested how to make ice cream, very quickly and with a little salt; that I should do well to get a shopping cart; and that he lived in the neighborhood -- I asked him for his name. "Bobby. And yours?" "Gerhard." Bobby and I will be friends, I am sure.

Roland and Florence Elliott

134

EPILOGUE

This story, like *Under the Crooked Cross*, is essentially the story of people and, in portraying them, of the signs of the times. Later perceptions, sometimes erroneously called wisdom, may well change earlier impressions and convictions.

Next to Heidi, Connie and Reni, the parents and Ray Maxwell were the most important people in the years 1946 to 1953.

Father retired from his parish ministry around 1960. He and Mother moved to a nice apartment in Emmelshausen, in the lovely Hunsrück hill country, some fifteen miles south of Coblence. They were comfortable, enjoyed good food and vacation trips with their little NSU car and by train; and visited us in Pottersville in 1961.

Father, never robust, lived to be 75; he died from pancreatic cancer or endemic anemia. Shortly before his death I visited him in the Stiftskrankenhaus in Coblence. He was quite pale and frail. He did not show his pain. He did not complain. Just before I left he thanked me, in uncharacteristically profuse sentiments, for having come all the way from the USA to spend a few days with him. Then suddenly, he turned to the wall, having said all he wanted to.

Mother outlived Father by nineteen years, to the day. For several years after Father's death she enjoyed a good, if solitary, life in Emmelshausen. Then, around 1981, when she could no longer take care of her household and herself, Richard -- and Connie -- moved her to an excellent old people's home near Lörrach on the Swiss border, over her strong protests.

One night, in the spring of 1985, her nurse realized that, suddenly and quietly, Mother's death was approaching. At Mother's request, she said a short prayer; and Mother said, amen.

Both parents are buried in that serene cemetery in Coblence, half-way up the Karthause hill and in the shade of tall sycamore trees, not far from where former generals of the Coblence garrison have their illustrious and martial monuments.

After five or six years with the World Council of Churches in Geneva Ray Maxwell returned to the USA, lived in Montclair, NJ, where Ilse taught some economics course at the local college. Ray eventually served as the top relief and refugee administrator at his own Episcopalian headquarters in New York. As neatly dressed and combed as ever, if a little grayer, the ribbon to the German *Verdienstkreuz* in his lapel, he and I sat together in a good many meetings of Church World Service committees; he always a thoughtful, modest and utterly loyal member.

Around 1970, in one of several down-sizing exercises, he lost his job, utilized his connections with the Church of the Rhineland and landed a pastoral assignment with a village congregation in the lower Westerwald. Ray retired several years later and he, Ilse and their Mercedes settled in the foothills of the Black Forest. In poor health for some years, he died in 1994. My carefully written letter to Mrs. Maxwell, remembering Ray as a good man and a good pastor, has remained unanswered.

As for me, I boast a bit: I am old, relatively poor, healthy and of good cheer. And I could perhaps say with that Chinese proverb: for a man to be a man, he must have raised a family, written a book and built a house. All of that, I have done.

Rather, and with more modesty, I should identify with Wilhelm Busch's state of mind and heart when he was my age. He was a cartoonist and doggerel poet around the turn of the twentieth century:

> I am done with my short biography. To be well rounded, the portrait should have had more reflection. But it did not seem fitting to use wonderful people whom I love and revere for purposes of self-aggrandizement. With regard to others less congenial, I have long since come to honor them with mild and steady silence.
>
> And so, here I stand in the deep shadow of life's hill. I have not become fretful but remained cheerful. Half smiling and half touched, I listen to the sounds coming from the other side of the hill where, in the sunshine, young people move forward and upward with laughter and their own hopes.

About the Author

Born in 1922, Gerhard Hennes grew up in Germany. He served in the German army from 1939 to 1946 and took part in the campaigns in North Africa, where he was taken a prisoner in 1943. As a POW he journeyed through sixteen camps in six countries. But most of this time he was confined in Crossville, TN.

After his return to war-ravaged Germany, he studied modern languages and is fluent in several. In 1947 he joined Church World Service, an American Protestant organization engaged in relief, refugee and development work. He has lived, worked and traveled in eighty countries. His fifty years in church work included six with the World Council of Churches in Geneva, Switzerland.

A U.S. citizen since 1958, Gerhard Hennes is a widower living in Fredericksburg, VA. His family is close-knit: two married daughters, three grown grandchildren and three great-grandchildren. He has restored twenty-one historical houses, a strenuous hobby. Besides three work-related books, he is the author of *The Barbed Wired* (2004), *Hybris* (2006) and *Under the Crooked Cross* (2008).

He now spends his time reading, writing, traveling and speaking. Gardening, fishing and landscape-painting are added in the summer. For an old guy, he says, life is good.